Be Cool, B-School!

Nishant Kaushik

ISBN 979-8-88935-865-7

Oh my God. This library, this dear old library was once home to our daylong endeavours of being the newest Counterstrike champions and to several late-night romantic rendezvouses in its nooks and crannies. Tonight, it looked like the abattoir I had once crossed in Juhu Gully. Only, the one hundred and seventy-five chickens here wore starched business suits, were too nervous to even cluck, and had put on several layers of perfume because nobody bathes during Placement Week. Yes, this is a tacit rule. If someone claims to have showered during this week, they are either untrustworthy or had not been exposed to the esoteric cure to our anxiety that Govind, along with his sugary, creamy tea, gave us a month before our big day. "DO NOT BATHE FOR SEVEN DAYS AHEAD OF GETTING A JOB."

"But how will we know what day we are going to land a job?" We had asked, circling him like followers beseeching their sage to dispense pearls of wisdom.

Expertly pouring equal amounts of tea into ten cups, he had smiled. "Faith. It will tell you."

Here we were now. Four days in, stinking AND still jobless. Thank you for nothing, Govind.

"Get me the CVs of the marketing batch. Now," Nilesh squealed into his walkie-talkie. Then, casting a glance at us so caustic that it could have burnt us if not for the air conditioner, he barked into it again. "Just the Day 3 people, I mean. Not the entire batch."

The Day 3 People. The outcasts. The nobodies who could not dance to Sukhbir's 'O Ho Ho Ho' on the quadrangle the previous night because they did not have an offer letter yet. The ones who kept getting patted on the shoulder and were told that it would all be ok because "after all, there will be something out there for you."

"You will be fine, Nakul," Nilesh put his walkie-talkie aside and hugged me. His affectation reached me even if his warmth did not. "Just don't be nervous."

Yes, easier said than done for the bloke who landed a 12L package with American Money Corporation on Day 0 and then marched the length and breadth of the campus to ensure that all two hundred and forty students as well as Silky, the stray cat that had merely snarled at us from a corner of the quad for two years, knew how much he would be earning three months from now.

"Bytesphere should be on campus any moment now. And trust me, they hire by the dozen. You are sure to get in there."

"Thanks, bro," I replied, deadpan and beat. "That does my confidence a world of good."

Bloody prick took it as a compliment. Not that I expected better from him. When I had scored a 2.86 GPA in the first trimester, he had followed me to the loo only to tell me that Professor Wankhede had reckoned nobody in the history of this institute had ever scored a 2.86. I had vowed that very evening as waste fluids escaped my raging body, I would raze Nilesh's arrogance to the ground. Like many other vows and dreams, this one had been razed to the ground too. If I had leisure time at hand right now, I'd take to a corner, mull over the twenty-one months I had wasted here, and undo some serious errors of judgement. Not least of those would be heeding Aryan's advice that it was only street-smartness, and not grades, that were going to propel our careers.

Flash Consumer Durables now arrived on campus. The giant projector facing us came alive. A hush of excitement rose in the room as people clutched onto yet another straw of hope.

'Are you game for Flash?' Aryan asked me. In the recesses of his mouth was a Happydent that had been working in overdrive to calm his nerves.

I circled my whitened face with my index finger. "What does this tell you? Do I look like I call the shots?"

"It is the attitude…" he began but stopped as soon as he saw my jaw drop.

"You – really, no really, Aryan," I shook my head in disbelief. "Even now you won't stop. So, anyway. Yes, I am game for Flash, Aryan. Do you think Flash is game for me?"

01

June 14, 2004. 8.40 AM.

I ran out of the shower, holding on to my towel for dear life. My head was a leaking thatch reeling from a thunderstorm. Fumbling for my papers inside a green translucent folder, I realised I had every document I needed at admission but had already failed the litmus test of a good MBA candidate the college had stated in its postscript.

Please be sure to report to the institute on time. Punctuality is the hallmark of every student we bring into our family.

Talk about being passive-aggressive. Slipping into the best clothes that had been purchased for my Big Day, I presented myself to the living room of the hotel's suite, where a housekeeper was clearing our breakfast plates as my parents sat and grumbled about the humidity.

"How long would it take us to get to Vile Parle from here?" I asked him nervously. "Twenty minutes, you reckon?"

His jaw dropped; then, realising the facial overtones of contempt and mockery wouldn't cut it, he placed the tray back on the table. Pushing his right hand behind his ear, he exclaimed, "Vile Parle! Twenty minutes? Sir, where have you come from?"

"Just tell us he is late," Papa suggested. "We will not be surprised on hearing that at all."

Mummy shushed him. "Don't be caustic. Not today, at least."

"Well, but he is right," said the housekeeper. My critics outnumbered my supporters. "In this city, you can't even get from Vile Parle to Vile Parle in twenty minutes, Sir."

"And how long does it take to get from Worli to Vile Parle – in this city?" Mummy prodded him.

He looked heavenward before lifting the tray again and making off. "Only God knows, Madam. One, one and a half hours?"

On cue, we bolted from the room and to the elevators, my luggage in tow, where my folks told me with amusement that repeatedly calling the elevator wasn't going to get us to our destination any sooner. The car arranged by the hotel waited for us in the lobby; its driver, dressed in a neatly starched uniform, opened the rear door for us. I was about to take the front seat for extra comfort, but then Mummy said I was already going far away from them and how much farther did I want to go that I was not even willing to sit with them for one, or one and a half hours? Therefore, I relinquished comfort and chose love, depositing my six-foot and eighty-kilos heavy frame in the middle of the sedan's rear seat. "Make it fast," I said as soon as the car revved to a start.

Maybe I should have said 'Please'. But no sooner had I spoken the words, than the smile drained from the driver's face and made way for a sulk. The car now trundled along the South and the suburbs at a snail's pace. I first thought he was doing this only to spite me or teach me an etiquette lesson. But when I opened my eyes and decided to deal with the anxiety and related nausea, I noticed the traffic lines were so long that the exit from one red signal only brought us to the tail of the next. It would be barely a matter of days before I realised 'making it fast' on the roads of Mumbai applied only to the preparation of Vada Pav.

"How do you always stay so calm?" I looked at my father, whose gaze caressed the congested skyline, a song from the nifty fifties on his lips.

"Why?" he shrugged. "I am not the kid who's getting late. I have every reason to be calm."

"I mean, at your job," I explained. "Being an IAS officer, working amidst crooked politicians."

"I do what I can," he said, patting my knee in kindness and reassurance. "But when things spiral out of control, and by God that is often, I just let go."

"But remember, he has learnt to let go only after he became an IAS officer," warned Mummy. "Don't learn to let go before you have made a fine life for yourself."

I sighed. "Does it strike either of you that I was never asked if I wanted to pursue an MBA?"

They exchanged nervous glances before Mummy turned to me again. "Do you want to pursue an MBA, Nakul?"

"Very timely," I retorted. The car had now reached Prabhadevi. To the right was the famous Siddhivinayak temple, towards which I muttered a silent prayer for divine intervention that would take me back home to Baroda. In the safe confines of my home where I could take as many weeks, months, and years to figure out what I wanted to do with my life while I splurged their hard-earned money. "What would you do if I said no, Mumma? Would we fly back home?"

"And do what, then?" Papa challenged me. "You did not score enough in school to get into Medicine. You barely passed Engineering. You don't want to pander to crooked politicians. You have vetoed all other career choices, Nakul. So, what would you do if we were to fly back home?"

"I forgot this world offers us only four career choices," I said under my breath, or so I thought because Papa caught on to it like a warrior ninja.

"All other choices are rubbish hobbies. Not careers."

I looked at Mummy for support. "Is this also what you tell your students at school?"

"Yes," was her flat response. "We should not have sent you to that career evaluation centre." Training her guns on my father, she said, "It was your grand idea. He wrote some essays there and they told him to pursue Fine Arts. Now he is questioning the two lacs we are paying for his MBA fees."

"Two?" the last time she talked to me about it, she said they had paid three. Their estimate of how much money had been shelled out for my higher education was about as accurate as a local's about how long it would take us from Worli to Vile Parle.

"Two, three, four, it doesn't matter," she slapped her palm on the college brochure I was holding on to. "Look here, son. This is it. You cracked the entrance exam. It only means you have the aptitude. Put your best foot forward for the next two years, and then the rest of your life will be sorted."

Famous last words. I had heard them during Class 10, Class 12, and Engineering. By now I knew this was at best a platitude meant to be nodded at. "Ok, fine. But did you see the picture of this college?" I placed my finger on the brochure. "A rather squat building with no campus."

"As long as there is a classroom that dispenses your lessons, you have nothing to worry about," she dismissed my concern.

"And the hostels are more than a kilometre away," I said. "The boys' and girls' wings are in opposite directions too."

"That is a blessing in disguise, trust me," said Papa. "That is one less distraction for you to worry about."

"You met Mummy when you were in college."

Words struggled to form around his mouth. When they did, they launched into a story. "When I was a little boy, my father once caught me exchanging class notes with a girl from my school. At dinner the same night, he glowered at me: *I will shoot you if I see you talk to a girl at school.* Consider it a privilege, son, that you take the liberty of teasing me like that."

"We are here, Sir," said the driver after more than an hour had passed since we first smelt the old upholstery of the car.

My heart thumped so violently now I feared it would rip my chest open. I noticed the logo of Fullerton Institute of Management Studies from two hundred metres afar: a Latin phrase about rigour and discipline, engraved within a shield-shaped emblem with a gold lining. I would not admit it to my parents, but a momentary sense of pride and gratefulness did creep into me.

"Drive into the porch," Papa instructed the driver. "And stay there – we won't be long."

I jumped out of the car and shut the door behind me. "Don't worry about getting down. I will find my way from here."

"Oh, no!" said Mummy. "We want to come and talk to your Dean."

"What for?"

"To see that the professors give you the attention you deserve, of course." Papa looked at me as though I had asked him to calculate the force of gravity.

I thumped the roof of the car, motioning the driver to move along. "No, that will not be necessary at all, thank you. Love you both!"

I did love them, I really did. But talking to the Dean of a post-grad institute to keep all eyes on one twenty-two-year-old man's ways of life was where I most certainly drew the line. After I was certain they had indeed driven out through the gate, I galloped clumsily into the lobby, my trolley bouncing on its marble floor until the noise gathered the attention of a watchman guarding the hallway.

He flicked his brows and held up a palm. "ID?"

"First day."

He examined the trolley and the fresh airline bag tag on its handle. "Follow me to the cloakroom. Don't lug that thing around or it will break your back. Do you know how late you are?"

He opened the door to a closet that had several other luggage items stowed inside, before answering the question himself. "More than an hour. Do you know what that means?"

Something told me he would answer this question himself too. I was right. "Rana Sir is going to take your case. Don't take it to heart. He claims one victim from the freshers' batch every year. Unless he has already found his scapegoat this morning, you are the chosen one."

"Where is Classroom 8?" I asked hurriedly. If Rana had to put me through the grill, I'd rather get it over and done with that very moment.

The watchman pointed upward and then took to the rickety stool he was on before seeing me. I darted upstairs, taking in the contrasting view of this building when compared to the gigantic acreage I had survived four years of Engineering in. There were no manicured lawns, just a cement-floored quadrangle with several sitting booths. Two stylised canteens with cool and funny graffiti made up for the lack of abundant space. The corridor was thin and long, with the library at one end and the only flight of stairs leading up to the classrooms and AV Room at the other. Somewhere in the centre of the lobby, was a noticeboard on which were pinned announcements for the senior batch and a list of two hundred and forty names from the new batch. And several fluorescent pamphlets listing rules and deadlines for the next business case contest, a cultural festival in the neighbouring college, and a Thought For The Day. Opposite it, the Dean's cabin was guarded by a large glass door. I ran up two steps at a time, finding myself thoroughly out of breath by the time I got to the big double door that guarded Classroom 8.

A bloke my age had beaten me to the race upstairs, his short but taut frame rising and falling to catch some much-needed breath as perspiration glazed his stubbled face. In his hand was a trolley too, with an airline tag just like mine. The poor fellow had lugged it two flights up, clearly missing an encounter with the watchman and his guidance to the cloakroom.

He pointed towards Classroom 8. "Are you…?" "Yes," I nodded in relief that I would not be the only one walking in late. "You too?"

"Yes, but I need to leave this somewhere first," he said, showing me his luggage.

"There is a cloakroom on the ground floor," I said, hearing which he instantly started running back down before I called out to him. "Hey, maybe we should report to class first?"

"Give me five minutes, will you?" he asked. "I can't be walking around campus with this luggage in tow."

"We are an hour late," I reminded him, hoping he'd see sense and get his priorities right.

"Oh, don't you worry!" he laughed, pushing the long curls of his hair to the back of his head. "This is not your typical college that takes you to task for being late every once in a while."

My response was suspect. "Really, how do you know?"

"I spoke to a lot of seniors and alumni. I have a lot of contacts," he said with a tinge of pride. "This is less of an institute and more of a party club. See how the quad lights up at night!"

"The seniors told you?" I asked again.

"Bet they did," he said, running along. "Ok, see you in five minutes. So just hang in there."

'Well, what were another five minutes against sixty that had already gone by', I thought. And at any rate, I'd take those five minutes over walking into that classroom and let the spotlight of shame fall solely on me.

And so I waited, observing that five minutes felt more like fifteen when under duress, and when he returned I observed he had taken fifteen, without a strain of remorse showing on his face.

"Sorry, I hadn't used the restroom since the time I boarded my flight this morning," he explained, pushing the door open. "Let's go."

As the door opened, it presented to us a hundred and eighteen eyes turning to us in unison. The deathly silence of that collective stare sent a shiver down my spine, but this guy looked as calm as a customer walking into a Barista to order an almond latte.

"May we come in, Sir?" he asked.

"This class or the next?" came the immediate counter-question.

Rana Sir was not what I had expected him to be, which was a rotund, irritable man who massaged his frail ego by ridiculing and chiding students half his age. He was instead a handsome middle-aged man with a neat crop of salt-and-pepper hair, a face with firm cheekbones atop a slender frame dressed in a polo shirt tucked into a pair of burgundy gabardine trousers. If he was not to be teaching us Economics, he would be George Clooney.

"This one, Sir," the boy next to me replied. "Sorry, we are a little late."

Or Ray Romano, if one judged him for his acerbity. "A little late? No, son. You are too early for your next class. What is your name?"

"Aryan, Sir."

"Aryan," Rana repeated. "Aryan, you have missed the ice-breaking session of my class where fifty-eight of your classmates introduced themselves to this group. The fifty-ninth, of course, is standing right beside you because *he is a little late too*. So, why don't the two of you take centre stage here and introduce yourselves to one another?"

Even in the heat of the moment, Aryan's sense of calm was not lost on me. In my grandmother's language, he was a *chikna ghada*, a slimy earthen pot devoid of shame. But in my world, his coolth was a trait I instantly aspired to.

Facing me, he extended a hand and a smile. "I am Aryan Nair. Formerly an RJ on Delhi's morning show, Delhi Talks. And you?"

Gosh. I lacked not only the coolth but also the necessary credentials to match his introduction. "I am Nakul. And I – well, nothing – I just finished graduation, and here I am."

"An RJ!" Rana butted in with excitement. "This is very unique, ladies and gentlemen. I want this conversation to continue. Someone get them two chairs NOW!"

Two eager beavers from the front row gladly gave up their chairs and came running to us with them. Reluctantly we took the seats offered to us as Rana approached Aryan.

"You must have hosted a fair number of guests on your radio shows?"

"Plenty, Sir," Aryan said with an air of harmless arrogance. "I once almost had the Union Home Minister over as a guest. But he had to cop out at the last minute."

"Good grief," Rana said broodingly. "Alas, you don't have the Home Minister today, but Nakul here is no less charismatic now, is he?"

I wanted to dig a pit in the earth and never be found again. If leaving home to pursue a course I was least inclined to was not enough, I had now allowed myself to be the laughing stock before a crowd of people I did not know until today and would be forced to be in the midst of for the next two years.

"Do a talk show with Nakul, Aryan," he said. "You have one minute. Make it interesting. Come on, your time starts now."

"So, Nakul," Aryan began, reclining in his chair and plucking threads off the torn fabric of his faded denim. "Tell us what brings you here?"

"What?" I looked at him, confused, irritated, faint – all at once.

"As in, what is your vision?" Aryan smiled, spreading his arms wide.

It may have been an innocuous question, but I took it as a slight upon my utter lack of vision as I stood at this strange juncture of my life. "Why, Aryan? Have you come here with a vision?"

"Of course," his tone suddenly softened to that of a sage who had just been kissed by the cosmic rays of the other verse. "To discover myself. To find what I am truly capable of."

"Ok that's it," Rana snapped. There was only so much meta-bullshit an Economics guy could withstand in an assigned lecture of two hours. "Thanks for the entertainment, boys. You may both leave now."

"But Sir," I pleaded. "Can we attend the rest of your class, please?"

"Try your luck in the next lecture," he shooed us away. 'And close the door on your way out.'

As the door shut on our faces, we heard Rana mutter to the class, "Who am I to interrupt their journey to self-discovery?" even as the others obliged with a round of laughter.

Having nowhere else to go before the commencement of the next lecture, we glided down the staircase so we could take to the canteen and cool ourselves off with a cola after the steamrolling we were put through.

"So your plenty of contacts from the alumni are not that reliable after all," I remarked as we settled on a table that had been freshly wiped clean with Windex.

"*Arre,* this Rana turned out to be a bad egg," Aryan clucked his tongue. "Don't paint the cultural fabric of this place with one broad stroke of judgement. I think we are going to have fun here. I can feel it in my bones."

"I am not here to have fun," I said sourly.

"Then, what are you here for?" he asked, laughter rising in his tone. "What is your – vision, Nakul?"

He ducked a tissue that I rolled into a ball and hurled at him. "Hey, look. Let this day slide. Ok, not the best start. Let us go to the beach this evening and unwind. Pretend today did not happen. We join this course tomorrow. Fresh ocean air, fresh perspective, a fresh lease of life – what say?'

"I say that's a brilliant idea," came a voice from behind me.

We turned over our shoulders to see two boys approach us. On the horizon, a crowd was streaming onto the quadrangle. Muted chatter was heard through the glass door fronting the café.

"Sameer Basu," said the boy behind the voice. "You can call me SB."

'*So much Bling*', I said to myself. Midas had probably bumped into him on his way here because SB was a walking pot of gold. Designer spectacles rimmed with gold, tiny piercings in his ears that looked like little balls of fire, a locket around his neck with his initials dangling off its rim. And he would never admit it, but the maroon shirt he had loosely tucked into his low-waist bootcut denim also had a little shimmer on it.

"You guys rocked it there in the class," he sat at our table, pulling a chair from the adjacent one. "The professor was so rattled by your brilliance he finished class fifteen minutes before time so he could go back and do some… what was it that they said, Swapnil? Yes, *self-discovery*!"

The boy next to SB, very basic in his countenance as though to offset the glitzy company he was keeping, simply smiled. A man of few words, but a smile with enough wattage to make up for it. His hair flopped onto his forehead, just short of his eyes. "Swapnil," he introduced himself. "Sameer and I had briefly interacted during our preparations for MBA entrance."

"And here we are now," said Sameer, slamming the table in triumph. "So, the beach tonight, yeah?"

"I am without a home right now," rued Aryan. "I have nowhere to keep my…"

"Luggage, yes," I said. "We must first check out our hostel."

SB pulled out a folded piece of paper from his pocket and uncurled it on the table. "We are two steps ahead of you. We have all the information you need."

The document listed a table with room numbers and their corresponding occupants, chosen by a random lottery system. I peered into the text. "You are Swapnil, right?" My finger coursed horizontally as I looked closer.

"Yes, and your roommate," said Swapnil. "I heard your name during your…introduction."

"And you and I are together?" Aryan now had the paper in his hand as he looked up at Sameer.

"Yes we know," Sameer grinned. "Did you really think we came to compliment you for what you said back in the room upstairs?"

02

"I did not think we'd be doing the graveyard shift even here," Vandana held her hands to her face in horror as she read the timetable on the noticeboard.

Monday: 1930-2200 hours: Organisational Behaviour: Faculty name- Prof. R. Siddique.

Soha giggled as she pulled her hair into a ponytail that would be held together by the hairband that rested between her jaws. "Graveyard shift, is that what they call 7.30 PM in Nainital?"

Vandana blinked rapidly, her tool to hide the exception she had taken on the joke about her home. "The call centre I worked in before I got here. In Delhi. Is that metropolitan enough for you?"

"Aww so sweet, touchy baby!" Soha rested her face in the hollow of Vandana's collarbone, giving her a tight hug. "Ok, Nainital is lovely. Call centre? You now have my attention. I have heard they have plenty of hot boys. Did you get it on with them?"

Vandana's almond eyes flitted anxiously to check for eavesdroppers. "Before marriage? Are you mad?"

"I am going to love your company, girl!" said Soha, her laughter rising with every response. "Ok come, let us go meet some cute boys. It has been three days already. You don't get it on with them ok? Just watch."

She led her into the café where they found us seated at the same table as always, our agenda vacillating between working on our group assignments and bemoaning the 4:1 gender ratio which had been observed by all of us but which affected only Sameer deeply, until he saw Soha march in and take the room by storm with her twinkling eyes, a scent of daffodils, and droopy blue earrings that matched the colour of her spaghetti top, perfectly contrasting her spotlessly white denim. "Who is she?"

"She is looking at you," said Aryan, without looking up.

"You don't even know whom he is talking about," Swapnil noted that Aryan had his back towards the girls. And at an intense level of Snake on his Nokia 6610, he couldn't be less bothered.

"Yeah but that is what Sameer would want to hear from us," he replied, furiously punching buttons on his handset, jumping a little every time he had a narrow escape.

"Why don't you join us?" Sameer waved at them suddenly – and without asking any of us at the table.

"He will make us all look desperate," I said, shaking my head in regret.

For all my judgement of his pomp and gaudiness, Sameer seemed to have a good success rate with 'Making A Move'. Because no sooner had he uttered the words the two girls started walking towards us. I'd consider that skill at any rate because I was now wholly and truly twenty and more, and had never mustered the courage in the seven years since I had sprouted my first facial hair to ask a girl to "join me" without any context for support.

"Division B, yeah?" Sameer asked them, pulling two chairs and extending them to them with the exaggerated body language of The Raymond Man whom we had not seen in the three days we had spent with him. "I am sure I noticed you both."

The frankness unsettled Vandana instantly as she puckered her lips in a wince and pretended to text someone on her phone. But Soha took the compliment as a matter of fact, without bothering herself with the formality of reciprocation. "I have heard that often, yeah."

At the introduction to her humility, it was clear to me that Sameer and she would hit it off like a house on fire. We exchanged names, some exchanged numbers, and that meeting would have been short and inconclusive had it not been for Soha's divulsion of critical information to us.

"I am a day scholar."

Sameer lunged at the opportunity as a langur would at food in the hands of an unsuspecting tourist strolling along the hills of India. "A day scholar, wow! I could use some company, then. You see, I am from Kolkata. New to Bombay, a bit lost but also very curious. Do you think you could show me around?"

"Not tonight, darling," she clucked her tongue. *Hmm, surely not something Sameer could have stomached hearing from a girl.* "But, later in the week, maybe? I get a lot of discounts at some clubs down South of the town if you guys are up for a dance one night?"

"I can see his feet tap already," said Aryan, smiling for the first time in the conversation. Pointing at his ragged off-white tee, he said. "We'd love to come too if a below-average dress sense is not a problem. Or else, I am sure Sameer can loan us some of his golden shirts?"

"Ha ha, funny boy." Laugh he did at the snark, but Sameer was not comfortable about a joke at his expense, surely not in the august company of the day scholar who, in his words a few hours and six drinks later, was the girl he was going to marry.

03

Six hours later, I was back in my hostel room, finding the next best way to deal with the mosquitoes that had ruined my previous night's sleep. Tonight, I had come prepared with the biggest tube of Odomos that sat on the shelves of the nearby pharmacy. And a resolve to tell Swapnil that a little bit of hygiene in the room never hurt anybody.

The room itself was not half as bad as I had imagined it would be. Where the founders of our university had pinched pennies by slapping three floors of concrete over two squares of acreage to accommodate a hundred and eighty boys, they had well compensated by designing our interiors with plush furniture, exquisite bathroom fittings, and aspirational views of bungalows and penthouses belonging to Juhu's rich and famous film actors, producers and industrialists. (One of our residents had claimed in the very first week he had seen Amitabh Bachchan step out onto his terrace to dry his towel after a bath. This claim was never validated but we all stood on the terrace every night for the next two years to try and corroborate it). My room though, looked like a ransacked godown, thanks to Swapnil's bed that had now become a makeshift laundry bed that he used to sleep on, open jars of sweet and savoury titbits that had become a festering ground for our ant friends, and his perennial absence from the room because of which I seldom remembered to call him out on the lack of order. Tonight was no different, I found, when I made enquiries with other residents I found strolling on the balcony.

"We saw him reading in the library," came the answer almost every day.

Must be into novels, I thought, because who in his or her right mind would be reading academic books before the orientation week had even ended. I made a note of items I needed to buy from the supermarket, a list including but not limited to a doormat, handwash, phenyl, naphthalene balls, and rat poison – the one that claimed would get rats to first eat it and then set out on a jaunt outdoors before breathing their last. For want of much company, I set out alone. The hallway was largely empty, except for a few guys sitting on the parapet discussing their experiences of the first week, or some of them in a corner or on the steps, smiling as they spoke over the phone to their love interests sitting far away, blissfully unaware that distance made hearts grow colder more often than fonder. Most of them were in their rooms, and the hostel was almost completely silent, except for the occasional sound of hard rock escaping a few half-open doors.

At the exit gate, I was stopped by a security guard who flipped me a register book.

"Sign." He pointed at a table drawn with his Reynolds ball pen. The columns included one's name, entry and departure times, whether we were entering single and exiting double or the other way round, and most interestingly – the reason for venturing out.

"Reason?"

He scratched his earlobe, acutely aware of the lack of purpose this information served. "Just write something."

Groceries, I scribbled and made off.

While I had no clear career goal, one thing I had become certain of: I wanted to make enough money to buy a home in the Juhu Development Scheme. There was a sense of calm about the whole area, as it was off the main road and away from the racket the rest of the city made. The houses had an alluring charm, the standalone bungalows in particular that were guarded by giant ebony doors and bougainvillaea creepers which, on the rare occasions that the gates were left open, would expose us to partial views of little manicured lawns and large swanky cars.

The streets of the neighbourhood were abuzz with activity at any given time of day or night. Senior citizens were seen marching towards Jogger's Park for their walks and laughter therapy and tea meetings. College students lazed around in bunches and couples, perched atop their cars, smoking out the day's fatigue, and gorging on their favourite pani puri and bhel puri at stalls that had mushroomed along several corners of its scores of streets. The market, a short and convenient walk from the hostel, comprised a series of shops that provided us with supplies, medicines, vegetables and fruits when we were tired of consuming junk food, and coffee shops that became a second home to us during late nights out.

But thirty minutes later as I headed back with my shopping bag in hand, I had to renege on my promise of settling down here. The sky was now pink and heavily overcast, signalling the arrival of monsoon. No, not the kind of monsoon that is romanticised in our films. The kind of monsoon that drains you with its humidity, has your clothes sticking to your body leaving weird animal-shaped sweaty imprints on your back and makes you run back to the market to buy half a dozen aerosols of deodorant, the use of which will now be in overdrive for the benefit of anyone who comes within breathing distance of your armpits.

Such as the security guard who stopped me again on my way back inside, with the same instruction. "Sign."

"Reason?" I asked again, to which he offered the same scratch of the earlobe, and so I wrote *Living here for the next twenty months* before taking the rickety elevator up to the third floor. Swapnil was now back on the mound of clothes that sat on his bed. His eyes were shut, and he sat cross-legged in meditation so deep it felt wrong to bother him, even if a part of me wanted to yank the clothes off from under him and chuck them into the wash cycle that very instant.

"Ah, when did you come?" he opened his eyes finally to the sound of my grocery bag being slammed on the study desk.

"I should be asking you that," I said. "I have been hearing reports about you disappearing into some corner of the library every night. What's up with that?"

He grinned, only on occasion, but when he did, they were generous and genuine smiles. "Usually, the library is for reading."

And the washing machine is for washing, I wanted to say but only managed to mutter, with no context whatsoever. "Hey, by the way, I just stopped by the laundry room and saw the washing machine is free to use. Just in case, you know..."

"Dinner?" he asked, looking at his watch.

Dinnertime it was. We went down to the lobby in the basement that was our dingy canteen, the perimeter of which was fenced by a semicircle of tables and spotty tablecloths, atop which were steel containers of lukewarm dal and two other gravies that did not look significantly different to the dal. Free food was a big incentive over the palate that brought all of us boys to the yard. We joined the beeline and were joined within seconds by Sameer and Aryan, who shared our absolute loss of appetite looking at the same food for the fourth night in a row.

"I have some sweet buns from home," Swapnil said. "Not the best dinner option, but do you guys want to give it a try?"

"And I have a crate of beer in our room," added Sameer. "A very good dinner option, say what? Shall we?"

We handed our plates to those who stood behind us and took to the terrace of the building, the door to which had a rather vague message stuck to it. *Do Not Loiter.*

"Does this mean we can sit here, at least?" we asked each other.

"Technically that won't be loitering, yes," we agreed and settled on the cold floor with our beers and buns, and of course, plenty of Odomos that would come in handy as the night grew thicker.

"So much better, this," we spoke of the starlit night that shone upon the boxes of cement and concrete slapped next to each other like cartons in a factory. Above them floated clouds of smoke emanating from the humongous city traffic that impeded a full view of the sea and beach at a slight distance. In time to come, the terrace was to be our regular haven for discussing our smallest of problems, venting our deepest frustrations, and celebrating our smallest achievements. The achievements were not as many, though.

"When the buns run out, will we have to go back to the same canteen?" I raised the first problem for the night as I sank my teeth into the softness of the dough. "These are delicious, by the way, Swapnil."

"Can your mother send more buns?" Aryan asked. "I could eat these every day for the rest of my life."

"What makes you so sure it is my mother who prepared them?" Swapnil tested him.

"Father? Sister?"

He smiled. "I did. And ergo, gentlemen, unless you get me a house here with a kitchen and an oven, you are not getting a new batch anytime soon."

"You've got to be kidding me," Sameer said in disbelief.

"He may not be," I spoke in support. "Our Swapnil is a Batman of sorts if you like. Slips into the library at night, sleeps on a mound of unwashed clothes with no fuss, and then whips the world some lip-smacking buns during the day."

"Another random reference to unwashed clothes in a matter of minutes," Swapnil observed me with the corner of his eye. "Are you trying to tell me something?"

"Oh, not really," my voice strayed away as I tried not to get overfamiliar.

"You can if you want," he laughed. You don't have to be so formal. I will wash my clothes when we go up. I know you have been itching to tell me that."

"I am glad we could be open about this," I gulped down a large sip of beer in relief, choosing to leave the discussion of the open jars of food for another day.

Sameer uncorked a beer, lit a cigarette, and took a generous swig and a drag. "Views, gents."

We followed his gaze to an apartment in the building opposite ours: a bedroom thronged by a group of girls our age enjoying a night out as they slouched on what seemed to be an L-shaped couch facing a large plasma television.

"Pyjama party," Aryan spoke with little to no interest. "Big deal. Do you ever talk about something that has nothing to do with women?"

Irked by the question, Sameer pushed himself against the water tank behind us and cocked his neck in a challenge. "Alright, RJ. Let us talk about something else. Choose a topic. Your kind is better at talking than I am. You do it all the time."

"Meaningless allegation," Aryan quipped coolly. What he had not noticed was that Sameer had already got on to his second beer for the night and he was only going to get more emotionally triggered from this point on. "Ok Sameer, let us take off from where Rana left us. Why are you here?"

"I was hoping you'd ask," he replied with a wink. "I am here to land a Marketing job with a leading FMCG firm. Marketing Director seven years from now. Maybe make CMO in ten? There's a precise answer for you. I have been carrying this dream since the time I started my BBA course three years ago. Easy transition."

There was an air of superiority in his words. Or it was his comeback to the accusation that he was hurting from because he went on to defend himself. "I know you guys think I only talk about girls. Not true. So don't judge me if you don't know my story."

This is usually the cue for us to ask someone their story. But the buns were delicious and the beer was chilled. So the interrogation could wait, we thought. At this sheer ghosting of his emotional outpouring, Sameer downed a few more cans and was now certified tipsy for the night because he rattled off in a single breath how his previous relationship in Kolkata unexpectedly failed and why he felt such a strong connection with Soha – stronger than what he had felt for Deepa.

"You have spoken to Soha for four minutes," I said. "I have limited knowledge on the subject but I can be certain that doesn't qualify as a connection."

"It is usually called a reaction on the rebound, isn't it?" Swapnil concurred.

Sameer was not well-positioned to take constructive feedback on the logic of his sentiments. "Where did I go wrong with Deepa?"

"Does anyone know the Deepa story?' Aryan whispered to Swapnil and me. "I genuinely want to help this guy, but…"

"We were together during high school," Sameer overheard the question. "Made for each other. We made tall promises to one another. But when the moment of truth arrived, only I held my end of the bargain. And when I confronted her about why she was ghosting me, she said I was invading her privacy."

"And, you weren't?" I asked cautiously.

'Subjective topic, this,' said Aryan. 'Invasion of privacy.'

"I was doing nothing of the kind," he wailed. "She just grew tired of me. New friends in Bangalore where she went to study Journalism. New friends, new focus. She grew tired of me. Dropped me like a hot potato."

"What does that have to do with you now trying your luck with Soha?" I asked.

"I told you – reaction on the rebound," said Swapnil. When offered a beer, he declined it. "Teetotaller, thank you. It helps me stay sane and see things the way they are."

Sameer couldn't hear our chatter, leave alone the volley of veiled sarcasm that had been hurled at him. "I am scared of losing her."

"Deepa?"

"To hell with Deepa," he snubbed us. "Let her have fun with her new friends in Chennai. I am talking about Soha. I hope she won't leave me."

"Soha has not even caught him yet," I slapped my forehead in protest.

"And Deepa is in Chennai?" Aryan asked, echoing our confusion. "A minute ago I heard him say Bangalore?"

"What does this tell you?" Swapnil asked Aryan with a smile.

"We need to carry Romeo to his bed," we said in agreement.

"And we need to do it now or else we aren't waking up in time for the Dean's beginning of trimester speech," Swapnil said worriedly.

"There is such a thing?"

"This institute is going to be full of surprises," Aryan shook his head.

"But how do we haul this chap up now?" asked Swapnil.

"When else will Aryan's biceps come to use?" I kneaded my knuckles into his arms, causing him to blush in acknowledgement.

"Been a while since I hit the gym," he smiled, pushing his sleeve down.

I rose, patting his back. Between the three of us lay Sameer, still murmuring something, yet asleep for all practical purposes. "The best workout is the one that happens in the now. Come on now, or we will miss the Dean's that-thing-he-said."

'How late are we?' I ran out of the shower hoping to find an answer, only to find Swapnil still buried under the comfort of his blanket, little snores audible when I stopped palpitating like a headless chicken. "Swapnil!"

He crawled out slowly. There was no sense of urgency about him, not a shred of anxiety when I told him we had but thirty minutes until the gates of the hall would close and the Dean's speech would begin. He sat on the same heap of clothes – no, he had not yet kept his promise of running the laundry – God, help me; he took three minutes to meditate, then another two to tell me that I must not worry and that he knew exactly how much time he needed to get ready. Before I could finish grumbling about the delay I would be subjected to on account of his callousness, he had emerged from the bathroom, running a comb through his poodle-like hair which if belonged to me, would have been chopped to a fifth by my mother one night when I was asleep.

"I hate asking, but did you not need to shower?" I asked uncertainly.

"We all do," he shrugged. "I did it at midnight. After we came down from the terrace."

"You shower at midnight?"

"Yes, I checked the hygiene box for yesterday as well as today with one visit to the shower," he bared his teeth in a chuckle. "What, you wanted me to save time, didn't you? Here you are. Now let's be off!"

We darted down the stairs; the elevator was so slow it felt like a carriage ferrying the Royals on a road tour. Five autorickshaws were lined up at a stand, seconds away from our building. One would have imagined hitching a ride would be easy as pie.

"Fullerton Institute of Management Studies?" we leaned into the first vehicle.

The driver, brandishing a toothpick on the corner of his mouth, shook his head. "Too close. I won't go."

We asked the next. The same shake of the head; yes, he had a toothpick too. "Too far."

"Seriously?" we looked at one another.

The third just shook his head but refused to oblige us with a reason. The fourth drove off just as we were about to duck our heads in to ask him the same question.

"Shall we just walk?" I asked.

The fifth, who had been privy to our struggles with the others, beckoned us with a whistle. "Where to?"

"Fullerton Institute of Management Studies," we said in identical plaintive tones.

He flicked his neck left, motioning for us to sit. Once we had sped off and he was certain we had no way of exiting his vehicle, he turned on a set of blue lights for some strange reason, and the radio to a decibel so loud it felt like a moving discotheque you could check out of any time you liked, but you could never leave.

"Reduce the volume," I demanded.

Again, the same old problem. I did not say please. Irately, he poked his thumb back at me. "When these two don't have a problem, who are you to complain?"

I looked sideward: posters of Preity Zinta and Kareena Kapoor to our left and right respectively, smiling their hearts out at us.

"I am giving you a deluxe experience," he said. "Not like those four useless fellows who declined to give you a ride. If anything, you should be tipping me at the end of your trip."

"Breathe in," Swapnil said to me, reading the rage in my eyes. "We are almost there."

By the time we reached college, we could no longer feel our ears. That was almost a nice thing because we had no inclination to listen to eight hours of back-to-back lectures on management principles and corporate discipline. But the hangover from the previous night was still working its effect, and keeping my eyes open during that mammoth day was going to be a formidable challenge anyway.

Aryan waved at us from a row sufficiently at the back for us to not worry about the odd snooze that caught us. "Over here!" he patted the empty chairs to his right.

"Not these," Sameer said with a start as we proceeded to take our seats. Placing a handkerchief on one of them, he said. "Take those two on Aryan's left."

"Who are these for?" I asked. As he returned a sheepish look, I sighed. "Sorry," I said.

"Am I smelling ok?" he asked me even as I sat down.

I leaned over Aryan to bring myself closer to him, despite seeing the absurdity of the question. "Say something?"

"Hello, Nakul."

"Ah, you smell like a rose," I raised my thumb in confirmation. "Talk to her with confidence."

He dabbed on some perfume and popped a mint for added measure. "I drank too much last night."

"We all did," said Aryan.

"But I was the one who passed out like a fool," he rued.

"Yes, won't deny you that claim," we said. "Now tuck your tummy in, they are here."

Soha and Vandana scampered in, seconds before the Dean was to take the dais. "Thanks for keeping our chairs!"

"Oh, my…our pleasure!" he smiled. Squarely ignoring Vandana's existence, he whispered to Soha. "You look great!"

She accepted the compliment with a playful pinch on his arm that magically snapped him out of his hangover. "Why, you flatterer, you!"

The brewing romance was cut short when we heard the knuckling of a mic. "Everyone quieten down now, please. We are going to start."

Dean Anil Mehra was a poker-faced man whose sadness, anger, rage, joy and ecstasy could never be told apart. And a monotone with acute ignorance of the use of a comma to boot, so he could sedate us and then pull us up for being sedated. It was all fun and games when it started. We were seated far enough to get away with the odd droopy eye, lobbing off the shoulder, and the clandestine exchange of notes that kept us engaged. He spoke of Corporate Social Responsibility, Corporate India – A Paradigm Shift, How To Avoid Procrastination and he was somewhere on Interpersonal Dynamics when the first full stop occurred, taking us all by surprise.

It was a very long full stop. He pursed his lips, and stood akimbo, his face still yielding no emotion. And then he bellowed. "Why don't you all sit from the comfort of your hostel rooms and hear me speak? Surely technology has advanced enough for us to still stay connected? Come on, go to your rooms, make yourself some hot cocoa, snuggle up in your blankets, and then I continue talking, yeah?"

It may have been our light-headedness but for a few seconds, Aryan and I did think he was serious. We were just lifting off our seats when a Senior from the Students' Council came running up to all the back-row enthusiasts. "Come on everyone, fill up the rows at the front."

Which is when we realised the importance of playing safe. Like a balanced mutual fund. When in doubt, do not take to the rows at the very back. Take the ones in the middle so that if a crisis occurs you are not pushed right up to the front to face the lion's wrath.

"Ask those snug bastards who are smiling at us," one of the backbenchers complained. "Look how they are looking over their shoulders and laughing at us."

"Dean Sir has called you guys out," said the Senior, now moments short of hauling us up by the collars. "They will stay where they are. It is you all who are not able to hear him."

We were herded now right at the front. To make matters worse, the Dean had now unleashed his trivia prop on us because he wanted to ensure we would not bat an eyelid. So he went about his topics in the same murderous monotone, but every few minutes he would pause, point a finger at one of us, asking us to summarise to the rest of the auditorium what he had just said.

"Tea break?" I hissed under my breath when I could take no more. "When is the tea break?"

He may have been a dull speaker but he was an astute listener. "Blue Shirt here wants to know when the tea break will occur. I am pleased to inform you that the tea break was scheduled at 10.30 for fifteen minutes." The sadist waited for us to exult before continuing. "But because we lost fifteen minutes in getting you laggards to fill up the spaces in the front, the tea break now stands cancelled. Any other questions?"

The exultation was replaced by a loud moan of protest that swelled him up with pride. "I am also pleased to inform you that lunch occurs at midday for an hour. Of this five minutes will now be deducted because I have spent that time explaining to you all why the tea break will not occur. Now – any other questions?"

And thus the torture continued throughout the day. The camels of Thar, and Dean Anil Mehra of Fullerton, it was astonishing how they could go so long without drinking a sip of water. At lunch, we were served delicious helpings of malai kofta, jeera rice and custard. While devouring the food we did wonder why this feast was such a stark contrast to the dal-lost-in-water that was being served to us in the hostel mess. Then we realised. Dean Mehra ate none of it. He only sauntered around the lunchroom chatting up all students while sipping on his holy concoction of warm water with honey. With a pat on the back, he egged us on to "Eat more, eat more," as he looked at us slyly. Sadist Mehra. He wanted us to be comatose with all the carbohydrates so he could slam us a little more in the second half. With our plates full and the food smelling delicious, there was no turning back now. Plus, free food. So we hogged until our bellies landed on our thighs and when the assigned fifty-five minutes of pigging it out were exhausted, we deposited ourselves in those depressing chairs like a bunch of gunny sacks.

The second half of the session was easier to tolerate because by now we had given up every effort to stay awake. We also observed that we were not the only ones struggling to escape the Dean's humiliation. Like a salmonella infection that passes on to all chickens once it finds its way into a coop, the Dean's wagging finger and an accompanying taunt found us all. Now with all of us equally awash with his denigrating comments, we were at ease and had already started making plans for the evening.

"Downtown tonight?" Soha whispered to us. "Vandana and I are going."

"Need you ask?" we said in response. "Anything is fine to unwind from the day we have had."

"Ok. But have you ever boarded a local train here?"

"How hard can it be?"

05

"Oh my God, no!" I broke into a sweat as Soha showed us a peek into the crowd waiting to board a train on the platform beneath us.

We had seen nothing like it. A sea of commuters formed an involuntary Mexican wave as they pushed and jostled and knocked each other over, preparing for the big fight. An announcement overhead warned everyone to keep a safe distance from the oncoming train until it came to a complete halt, the blaring of a train horn in attestation of the warning. But the crowd paid no heed to the advice because there was indeed nothing like a 'complete halt'. The train slowed, people jumped out, people jumped in, and the train moved again before we could even finish saying 'What the hell was that'.

"Relax," she laughed, walking us down to the other side of the footbridge. "This train was northbound and hence a bit busier in the evenings. We are going against the traffic tonight."

That was little solace because we now found ourselves amidst a crowd not significantly smaller and definitely not any less belligerent. We felt elbows, body odour and fingernails that mistakenly scratched our faces instead of those of their owners. As well as these, the two girls with us also received the evergreen gift of the male gaze as they stood next to us in their formal pencil skirts.

"What is it, Uncle?" Vandana finally turned to a man who was now dangerously close for comfort. "Have you never seen a skirt before?"

"That's my girl!" Soha slapped her back, turning to all of us. "She is now anointed as a local of Mumbai. Your move now, gentlemen! Here we go!"

The train arrived. The challenge had been laid out. We rolled up our sleeves and geared ourselves for The Big Push.

"Now!" cried Soha, and on cue, we pushed, tugged, elbowed, knuckled and tickled everyone around us. Ten seconds felt like an eternity but we ultimately did get in, mostly thanks to the restless people behind us who carried us in.

"And the anointment is now complete!" Swapnil exclaimed once we had found a spot in the bogie where we could stand and breathe.

"I won't say that about Nakul," said Soha. "I heard him say *Excuse Me* while trying to get in."

"Rubbish," I protested.

"Don't deny it," she argued.

"Seriously?" Sameer laughed.

"Ok, so I did," I admitted. "And then I took it back."

"It stays with you," she said. "We will now always know you as the chap who asks to be excused at the local station."

"Not a bad thing, honestly," Vandana came out in my support. "A nice oddity in an unruly crowd. I am with you, Nakul."

"See?"

"Very well," relented Soha. "So you have passed the Local Train test. Now to get you all soaked in the dining and nightlife culture of South Bombay. What food do you feel like?"

"Anything better than what we have been eating in the hostel," I said.

"No, as in," she paused to explain. "Pick a category. There is the Collegian option – your roadside meals-on-wheels, cream corners, juice and bhel stalls. And then there is the sophisticated option: the fine dining restaurants, the clubs where you will bump into the high and mighty and smell their perfumes."

"Oh, the sophisticated ones," Sameer voted immediately.

"Are you paying?" Aryan asked him.

"Of course, he is," Vandana chimed in. "His suggestion, his wallet."

Nothing spectacular or out of the ordinary happened over the course of the next thirty minutes. We stood by the window like six wax statues in a closed circle such that the perspiration of a seventh human would not drop on our shoes. From the mills dotting the twilight horizon, an unsavoury odour of chemicals and soot wafted in. People spoke loudly and people spoke softly. A boy in his early teens, accompanied by his little sister, played *Tere Mere Sapne* on his flute as she complemented his music with an accurate rendition of lyrics. But the train ride and the associated discovery of a new city and new friends became the cornerstone of my memories of my MBA. Not Kotler, not Six Sigma, not the Principles of Macroeconomics. In time to come when I drifted into self-doubt or homesickness or was in unrest because I feared for my future, I went back in time to this bogie and the frames and fragments I captured of the night: the dinner we ate, the music on the boy's flute, the chatter about little nothings we busied ourselves with through the night by the beach.

Sameer would remember it for a different reason, I reckoned, because of what transpired when the cheque arrived at the end of our dinner at the upmarket Gaylord's in Churchgate.

"1940, thank you," the steward slipped it right in the middle.

With heavy hearts, we were fumbling through our purses to let loose three currency bills of a hundred each and one score, when Sameer held Soha's hand in an unsolicited gesture of chivalry.

"Let it be," he said coyly. "It is on me."

"How sweet, Sam!" she readily agreed, and in reciprocation had offered him a nickname too.

Aryan seized the opportunity and shoved his own wallet back in his hip pocket too. "Yes, how sweet, Sameer! True pal."

"What, I didn't mean to," he began.

But the horses had bolted. "Thanks, chum, owe you one," said Swapnil.

"You really took this seriously," I said. "Thanks, man."

"1940 is a lot, Sameer, are you sure?" Vandana asked. "Well, next time's on us, yeah?"

"I can't wait until next time," he grumbled under his breath while placing his credit card on the table. He'd deal with his father's enquiries about the bill later. At this time he cared more about not looking like a clown in front of the girl he was busting all chops to woo.

We walked along the perimeter of Marine Drive, soaked in the elegance of The Queen's Necklace, and gorged on *Bachelor's* Strawberries & Cream for dessert in the dead of the night.

"What class do we have tomorrow morning?" someone asked when we had run out of topics to talk about.

"You mean today," Swapnil corrected the question and then looking at his watch, clarified. "As in, three hours from now? Financial Management."

"Good Lord," I sighed, laying down one final time for the night on the softness of the cold beach sand.

06

"How many of you have studied Accounts before, at whatever level?" was the first question Prof. Biswas posed to the class. A couple of dozen hands went up instantly. "Well, that's a much better number than I had expected! This batch seems to have a healthy proportion of commerce graduates. So I presume I can run through the basics a little fast, am I right?"

I felt queasy. I hoped someone would stand up and protest. Someone like me who had never seen a balance sheet before. But nobody rose, and I did not want to be the only dumb coot to raise my hand.

"For the uninitiated," he continued, "I am sure your friends will always be ready to help you out with the basics. And of course, my door is always open for you whenever you need help."

He ran through a brief explanation of the contents in a balance sheet at the speed of lightning. By the time I could draw the balance sheet table in my book, scribble "Assets and Liabilities" on the top of the page and stomach the terminology Prof. Whirlwind Biswas was rattling off, he had already moved on to "Calculation of P/E ratio" and some other such terms that gave me instant acidity. Desperate, I began to peep into the notebooks of students around me, hoping to find a lead that could get me going.

"Struggling?"

Groggy from the unplanned night out, I had failed to notice her despite sitting right beside her. The others I usually paired up with in the classroom had not even attempted to wake up and make it to class. And so I had found myself whatever vacant spot I could, and now that she had asked me a question, I felt compelled to check her name printed on the I-card that lay on our table.

"Um yes…Naina. Struggling."

I would have thought this question would be followed by an offer to help. I could also see she was well-equipped to help as she was comfortable with her debits and credits. But she did not look up from her notes once, her square-rimmed spectacles nearly touching the tip of the paper she was working on.

We had now been handed an assignment. Wow, this was all happening very fast. Biswas was now doing rounds up and down the aisle to see how we were getting along, and the only text on my page was the name of the subject he was teaching.

I peeped into her notes. Blind copying was better than doing nothing. "I am an engineer," I told her. "These numbers…"

"They sound like Greek and Latin to you." She pre-empted my difficulty. Again, an accurate observation but no offer of help.

"Seems like a piece of cake to you," I said. "Very impressive."

"This is basic stuff," she replied, still not looking me in the eye. "Nothing to be impressed about. It should be a piece of cake for everyone."

Ok, so this was it. Immodesty is where I would choose to draw the line. "Very well, then."

Biswas passed by my seat shortly after. Thankfully he asked me nothing and did not do a Rana on me. Once he glided on to other desks, I heaved a sigh of relief and looked for other ways to keep myself occupied for an hour. The most interesting way would be to find a comeback for Naina who had tried to show me my place.

Looking for a clue, I eyed her I-card again. Date Of Birth: 19th June 1980.

"Three years longer on this earth than I have been," I said. "That extra time should count for something, shouldn't it?"

I finally had her attention. Placing her pen down, she looked up at me. Her steely eyes pierced me through her numbered glasses. "So, you are saying I am better at accounts because I am three years older than you?"

"Well, there is merit in the argument."

"Which means you are not only bad at accounts, but you are also ageist?" She asked with a smirk.

"Just factual."

She shook her head. "Don't have a go at my age. You will be my age in three years." She mulled, tapping her pen now on her square jaw. "Oh, you can pick on my height. I get that a lot. Do you see this?" She pointed at a cushion she was seated on. "I carry this wherever I go so that my face can reach my desk. You can thank me now, what's-your-name. I have given you an idea."

Our words had now reached Biswas. He turned back sharply and spotted us, giving us the stink-eye. While I was doing nothing productive sitting there, I had no inclination to be asked to leave the class a second time.

"I am sorry," I whispered. "About the…ageism. Ideas on how I can make fun of you were not the help I was seeking, though."

She dug her head back into her books, turning away from me in what I thought was resentment. But at the end of the class when the books were shut, she turned to me again. "I will be in the library from six to eight this evening. Feel free to drop by. I can teach you some basics."

She left without waiting for me to say 'Thank You'. I decided to take her up on the suggestion anyway rather than deal with the anxiety of passing a Finance exam in three months. The rest of the day gave us an introduction to Marketing Management and Organisational Behaviour, which in comparison felt like a cakewalk. It is Finance that had me by the throat. Hoping to clear my mind and draw out a plan to prepare for the trimester tests, I took to the library earlier than the appointed time.

And I drew out a plan. Sadly, only on paper. Titled 'My Academic Plan – Trimester 1' with a lot of bullet points and daily reading schedules, magazines that I would read, market research that I would conduct, and voluntary assignments that I would take up for a panoramic understanding of all subjects. History should have told me that such plans were seldom adhered to. But then they always made me feel good on that day, and that evening I contended with feeling good.

I was browsing a handbook on Accounting for an augmented feel-good experience when I was greeted by a slap on the back.

"Oh, look who is studying hard!" Aryan and Sameer stood behind me.

"We have a week to submit our first assignment," said Aryan. "Why are you sitting here already? We are in this together, ok?"

"We are?" I asked, perplexed. "Anyway, I was not doing much. Just waiting for Naina to come and help me recap what Whirlwind Biswas taught us this morning."

"Who is Naina?"

"And who is Biswas?"

"Naina is someone who knows Financial Management a little better than I do," I said. "And Biswas is the one giving me nightmares on Financial Management right now."

"Ok now, important announcement," Sameer said, closing my book. "We are hitting Enigma tonight. Let's go."

"Sorry," I opened my book again. "Financial Management it is."

Aryan tugged at my collar, trying to lift me. "Are you really going to prefer the company of an Accounts nerd over Juhu's trendiest nightclub?"

We heard the clearing of a throat. Naina stood behind us, three books cradled between her folded arms. Stepping towards Aryan, she extended a hand. "Hi. Accounts Nerd."

"I am so sorry," he stammered.

"That's fine," she shrugged. "I have been hearing things about myself all day. Learn something new daily, they say, yes?"

"Good things," I hastened to add. "Isn't it? I was just telling Sameer and Aryan how you have so kindly…"

"No, no, I shouldn't have said Nerd," Aryan insisted. "Deeply offensive. Naina, would you like to join us at a club tonight?"

"Sameer? Did you say Sameer?" she asked, looking at both of them.

"That will be me," Sameer waved.

"Ah, then the club would have been a good idea,' she smiled for the first time since I had seen her. 'Because I have heard of your large-heartedness when it comes to footing big bills."

Ashen-faced, Sameer stared at us in accusation. "You rascals! Have you broadcast this already?"

"No, they haven't," she replied. "My roommate was the beneficiary of your kindness. She could not stop talking about how much she is looking forward to dining out with you again."

"Oh my! News spreads," he groaned. "Vandana has been a magpie."

"There were four other girls in our room when she told me," she said with a wink. "Now don't lose your marbles over such a small matter. Go have fun at the club. I will give it a pass. I am not even dressed for the occasion."

She ran a palm down her black Reebok T-shirt over a pair of loose track pants of the same colour. In her feet was a pair of floaters. Surely a no-go for Enigma.

"Same here," I reaffirmed.

Having seen the boys off, I returned to my seat. "Alright then, let's deal with this phantom. Begin with the A-B-C of the subject, will you?"

She raised a hand to stop me. "Before we even go to the A-B-C, stop calling it a phantom. Or else you will learn nothing."

"Ok, noted."

"Yes, so I know a little more than you," she admitted. "But that is because I worked two years at my brother's accounting firm before coming here. That is not to say I wasn't in your position before that, yeah?"

"Ah, family business!" I said. "What else does one need?"

A scoff took over her tone. "Yeah, right."

"What do you mean?" I asked. "Am I wrong?"

She poked a finger in my book. "This is what we are here for, kid. This is what we are going to talk about."

I might have touched a nerve. I stepped away from the question and got on to the A-B-C. She spent over an hour ramping me up to the final assignment Biswas had left me with. The hour left me with minimal enlightenment on number-crunching, but it found me a new friend.

"And a guarantee that you will pass the exam with flying colours," she said as I prepared to leave.

"I will owe you one if that happens," I said. "By the way. Are we friends now?"

"Only if you take no more digs at me," she leaned back, gauging my next potential reaction.

"I just don't think you are that short," I said. "Or old."

She laughed. "Just the validation I was looking for. Thank you!"

"And sorry if," I paused to wonder if I ought to be going there again, but then did anyway. "Sorry if I said something you did not like. About your family business."

At this, she stood up abruptly to leave. As she walked past me there was a tensing of the jaw, a welling up of the eyes. A desperation for stoicism in the face of despair.

"We can talk," I called out weakly. "Only if you wish."

She turned around. Fighting back tears, she asked. "Do you want to go out for coffee sometime next week after class?"

07

The first shower of the season filled us with childlike joy. The humidity that had got my goat the first time around was all but forgotten. We were too old for paper boats, but the roads awash with rainwater looked inviting and we set out on an all-boys walk. Dressed in ragged shorts and worn-out jumpers bearing stains of chutney and toothpaste, we set out – four friends, and Aryan's Gibson guitar.

"You did not tell us you play!" Swapnil said once we had settled on the beach, ready to jam.

Juhu Chowpatty wore an unusually deserted look that evening. Save for a few kids playing cricket by the waves in a corner, the residents had taken cover under the forewarning of heavy showers. The skies had turned a mystical grey that bordered on black. The waves crashed furiously at the shore.

"Perfect setting to tell you all I do," Aryan smiled as he tuned the keys on his headstock. His hair tied back in a bun, he shut his eyes to find a moment of inspiration before he started strumming. Building a gradual rhythm, he explained. "Music is the only love that does not leave you. It stays. See what I mean?"

We did not see what he meant. It sounded like a line straight out of a speech on Aastha TV. We only wanted to sing at this opportune location where the only audience that would have to tolerate our cacophony was three stray dogs growling at us from a dozen feet afar. One song followed another, interspersed often by our ad hoc requests. Aryan obliged each with a nod and a smile, knowing the perfect note and chord and pace at which each song must be played. Guitaring came easy to him, we told him.

"You must be the first guitarist who does not use his guitar to become the centre of attention," I said.

"Yeah, girls love a man with a guitar," Sameer agreed.

"You have never held a guitar," Aryan replied. "But girls love you, don't they?"

"Do they?" I asked. "Who is in love with you, Sameer?"

"Arre, just tell him what he is keen to hear, will you?" Leaning into my ear, Swapnil whispered Soha's name.

"Rubbish."

"It is not," Swapnil said. "They have started going out on dinner dates. How many has it been, Sameer?"

"Who is counting?" Sameer asked, blushing as he drew circles in the sand around him with his finger.

"Your credit card is," said Swapnil.

"Don't tell me!" I rolled my eyes in disbelief. "You are still footing the bills?"

Seeing Sameer twitch with displeasure at the unsought lecturing, Aryan snapped a finger. "Guys! Music, please. Ok? I need an attentive audience."

Our private concert progressed for another hour and a half until it was interrupted by a noisy ringtone on Sameer's phone. Springing to his feet, he scooted to answer it and did not return for the next ten minutes. From a distance, we saw him strolling up and down a metre worth of beach sand. A smile of satisfaction adorned him as he nodded, spoke, and then nodded some more.

"Any guesses whose call that was?" I asked.

"Can I answer that with a song too?" asked Aryan.

"Only makes it better."

When I was just a lad of ten, my father said to me

"Come here and take a lesson from the lovely lemon tree.
'Don't put your faith in love, my boy,' my father said to me
I fear you'll find that love is like the lovely lemon tree!"
We joined in.
"Lemon tree, very pretty, and the lemon flower is sweet.
But the fruit of the poor lemon is impossible to eat!"

Sameer returned presently, only to tell us he needed to leave. "Soha needs to go shopping on Hill Road. She does not have company."

"She was born and brought up here," I told him. "She must know half the town, half of which can give her company."

"So?" he asked with a hint of irritation. "She has asked me. Is there a problem?"

Aryan placed a hand on my shoulder, motioning for me to stop. "Carry on. We will see you tonight, yeah?"

"No, out with it," Sameer insisted. "What was that about, Nakul?"

"Doesn't matter," Swapnil interjected. "Do you love her, Sameer?"

"Seriously?" I laughed.

"The question is to him," said Swapnil.

"Yes," he said. "Yes, I do."

"That's great, then," I said. It was not my place to interfere in his personal matter. "I just wondered if it was too quick for you to decide you are in love with her."

"This feeling has nothing to do with time." Sameer now had his hands over his hips in defiance. "Your logic is absurd."

I raised my hands in the air. "Sorry. I should not have brought it up. Carry on."

Long after he had left, a strange disquiet engulfed us. Aryan distracted himself by lightly strumming a song he had composed. Swapnil fiddled with his mobile.

I felt uncomfortable and at a need to justify my pestering. "There is something about Soha that has SHREWD written all over her."

"Yeah, I know," Swapnil said.

"So? Why did you not say it?"

"There is no prescription saying you cannot love a shrewd person," he replied. "Let him be the judge of how to handle his love for her."

"Yeah sure," I said, stretching on the cool ground beneath me, letting out a yawn. "As long as she loves him back, no dramas."

"Dude! This is where you are wrong," Swapnil laughed. "He can't love her on a guarantee of return. That's not how it works. You have no experience, do you?"

"Oh!" I goaded his knee with my bare toe. "I am talking to a man with experience. Tell us your story, Lover Boy!"

"Not to you, no," he pulled away. "You apply too many checks and balances on the whole emotion."

"Ok sorry," I said. "I won't. Tell me your love story."

"Some day," he said.

Aryan looked up finally, as though snapping out of a dream. "What are you guys talking about?"

"Waiting for your next song."

We sang John Denver's *You Fill Up My Senses*. Midway through the verse, I reflected upon my preachiness. When and why did I become this person who could not mind his own business to save his life? I would apologise to Sameer when I met him next. I would tell him that Soha was a lovely girl and the two of them together were like a house on fire. I would promise to always stay in my lane.

08

Three hours after having apologised to Sameer, I was back to playing an expert on Relationship Advice. I could not help it even if I wanted to. It felt like a newly acquired superpower that crept into me with an overwhelming itch hard to shake off.

I reached the coffee shop at the appointed time of a quarter past eight. The cows had come home, our professors had gone home, and the rains were pissing down on the city with a rage so blinding, one had practically no vision of things three feet ahead. The Barista outlet was a quaint corner tucked beside the beach with six tables placed equidistantly along its length. Four of them on any given day were occupied by students like me who found more purpose in life outside campus than on it. One was always dedicated to an aspiring actor that had finally fixed a meeting with a 'top director' who had agreed to this meeting not to offer a role but to offer the newbie unlimited career counselling with free refills of black coffee. The last table was reserved for the odd bunch – a teenager's parent who had called an ad hoc coffee outing with their rebellious offspring in the hope to break the ice while breaking bread.

Naina arrived minutes after I did: I recognised her from across the road despite the extra-large raincoat that fit on her petite frame like a scarecrow's shirt. Her jeans were rolled up above her ankles. Her favourite floaters held her tonight in good stead, resilient against the puddles of water she stomped through after paying for the autorickshaw. She waved at me through the glass façade as she folded the soaked umbrella, carefully ensuring that the residual water from its fabric landed only in the bed of plants lining the walkway.

Placing the umbrella in a bucket that had been placed at the entrance, she approached me gingerly to avoid slipping on the wet marble floor. "Hi," she said, enveloping me in a hug. "Did you have to wait long?"

"Lesser than you will have to wait for me if we meet often," I smiled, offering her a seat. "I am usually late."

"But you were on time for me," she said, taking her purse out. "Coffee is on me then. What will you have?"

"Oh no, we will go Dutch," I said, getting up, but she pushed me back on my chair.

"An extra-hot Mocha then, please." I might have been a wuss for complaining about non-existent things like Mumbai's cold weather. But the monsoon had brought with it a biting chill that my Gujarat-tuned body dressed in a drenched Lacoste T-shirt and damp denim was refusing to accept.

She returned with a mocha and lemongrass tea. "Extra hot, like you asked."

I took a sip and exhaled as the warmth made its way through my veins. "I feel so much better."

She took off her raincoat and placed it on the back of her chair. Behind us, vehicles crawled and honked. Cyclists zipped past them, having the last laugh on a night that had brought all large vehicles to a grinding halt.

"Thanks for coming," she said, taking the first sip of her tea. The drink was hot; it gauzed her tongue and she struggled to speak for a few seconds.

"Are you alright?" I asked, pouring her a glass of water.

"No!" she spoke in a tone stuck somewhere between laughter and pain. "No, I am not okay. My tongue just got burnt, I have no friends here and my family…"

She took large sips of water and breathed a sigh of relief. The tea had to be set aside until it cooled. "My family is not proud of me. If that answers your question from the other day."

She buried her face in her hands and began sobbing. I ran to her side and placed my arms around her. It was the only thing I could do, and it was not until then, that I truly understood what it meant to be by someone's side. A single child whose growing years had seen the comfort of a bureaucrat's household, the company of equally carefree friends, and a teenage that was offered a long list of luxury holidays, I had not really smelt strife and despair. If there was one thing I had missed, it was the presence of a sibling – an option of sharing my deepest desires and largest fears, of squabbling with someone without the fear of losing his or her loyalty. Or simply being there for someone.

No one needed my emotional support. Until now. And at that moment when I held her by the shoulder, I smelt strife and despair. "I am here," I said. "Tell me everything."

I dragged my chair closer to her and waited until she had calmed down. "Your tea."

She felt the rim of the cup. Tentatively, she took a small sip. Certainly not boiling hot now. "That job at the accounting firm? I had to fight for it more than I probably would have to if I sought a role outside the family business. Simply because the family did not want me there. I went to the best school in Calcutta. Did exceedingly well at college. It was only in the final year that I would learn it all amounted to nothing. Because in our tradition, the family business is handed over to the scion. And the girl is married off. There is no exception to the rule."

"Until you made an exception."

"My brother supported me," she said. "Thank God for that. He fought with my father and said if an internship at the firm is what Naina wants, then she has a right to it. Look, my brother fighting my father's views is very different to me fighting them. They get angry with him, but that anger slides over. In my case though, there is no room for errors, let alone rebellion."

"Are your parents not in touch with you now?"

"See, that is the very problem," she said. "If they hated me and had disowned me by now, I would at least know there is no going back. But this blowing hot, blowing cold is killing me a little every day. They won't let me go, but they won't hold me either. I live with them. I will go back to them every trimester holidays. I will be fed and given gifts on Diwali, but they will leave no stone unturned to let me know how much I have disappointed them with my decisions."

"That might change once you graduate from here," I said. "Justify the expenses you have incurred being away from them."

"There are no expenses incurred," she said. "I am supporting my fees here with whatever I earned at my brother's firm. But that just infuriates my father even more. I know he loves me, he always has. I was always the spoilt one. I was always allowed to take liberties with him. Disobedience was just not one of those liberties."

Four more coffees were ordered. At the end of a long evening, I found a new friend whom I thought I understood better than the ones I had grown up with.

"What did you mean you don't have any friends, though?" I asked as we headed back. The rain had mellowed to a drizzle, so we decided to ditch the autorickshaw and walk back to our hostels. "I am one, right?"

"The first, yes," she replied, patting my back. "One is a good start."

"And the others," I added. "You already know Vandana. And Aryan and Sameer. You have not met Swapnil, but he is a gem."

"And they will be ok with me hanging around?"

"Yeah, we don't really do interviews!" I laughed. "You are inducted. And you will be joining us tomorrow at the cinema. Get it?"

"Deal," she smiled.

We stopped at the girls' hostel. She gave me another hug before stepping in through the side gate left open for 'after-hours' entry. "Thanks for being there."

I had really done nothing other than exist in the same radius as hers when she let her heart out. The occasional nod and the *yes* and the *I understand.* I understood little about her world then. I was in a position to help even lesser. But her words and gesture had elevated me to a position I would find hard to relinquish – an indispensable friend who had sealed a permanent contract of friendship with clauses that included reciprocation on demand.

The party had come to a sudden pause. Exams were around the corner and the entire batch was slogging late nights after classes in the library. I had not sensed I was underprepared until I saw Swapnil, Naina and Vandana huddled in a corner one night helping each other revise lessons with fervent passion. I sat with them for ten minutes, which was enough to knock the wind out of my sails.

I remembered nothing! I was drawing a total blank on every word they had just discussed. This could not be happening to me. Were those different textbooks, a wrong curriculum, a wrong course altogether that I had been reading up all these weeks? Or was it just the 'fresh air' that I used to step out for during my study breaks into which all my learning had been steadily evaporating? I felt my stomach churn. Looking around the library, I desperately hoped to see *one* face that appeared as petrified as mine. And then I saw Aryan biting his nails in the corridor.

"Dude, this Economics is killing me," he admitted upon finding me approaching him for help.

"I will say that about every subject," I gasped. "What do we do now?"

"*Let's study* would be an obvious answer," he said.

We took to the Amateurs' Corner in the library, a table on the floor above where we could try reading our course material with some much-needed focus. But in less than an hour we had figured out that the motivation to survive this week ahead of exams did not lie in the closed rooms of our library. "We are doing this wrong," said Aryan. He popped spearmint in his mouth. Chewing on it, he spoke. "Let us share the load. Have you heard of the fable about the miser who insisted all his guests at dinner could only eat without bending their elbows? The guests extended their arms and fed one another, man. That…"

"Aryan." I showed him a tense frown, holding up my hand. "Time is of the essence. What's your point?"

"Team spirit," he said. "We need that team spirit."

"So, we go and feed each other?"

He sank his head in despair. As though I was the one going around in circles. "No. We have fourteen chapters to cover. You read the first seven, I read the latter seven. Then we summarise our respective chapters to the other. There is no way we can read and digest all fourteen."

If this plan had been offered by someone else, I would have called bullshit on it. But Aryan had the confidence and the nonchalance of the weatherman in a newsroom when he handed this proposal to me.

"Surely you must have tried this before," I asked, just to be sure.

He slapped me on the back and said, "It works like a charm. Come now, cheer up. Let us swing into action!"

We took to the library and learnt by rote every word of the seven chapters we had assigned ourselves. When there was something we did not understand – which was most of the time – we created lame analogies and acronyms, then laughed at our ingenuity because we thought we had conquered the world. At midnight we were high on overconfidence. Like a dash of marijuana that sends you floating amongst the clouds, our marathon session in the library (two hours was a marathon for us) had convinced us we were getting an A+.

"Alright," I said, shutting my book in victory. "Who is going first? Do I summarise the first half to you or the other way around?"

"Neither," he declared. He slipped on a faded denim jacket, undid his bandana to let his hair down, and pulled me by the elbow. "At this point, we take a strategic rejuvenation break. Give our minds some rest. The recapping then works like magic."

He assuaged the suspicion reflecting in my eyes with the two words that now felt like a potion. "Trust me."

Hence we set out for our strategic rejuvenation break. First for a walk, followed by a drink at Toto's, topped up with egg-pav outside Cooper's. Over the course of this break, I was exposed to Aryan's joie de vivre and was so heavily influenced by his devil-may-care attitude that I had come to surmise that failure was only a state of mind. He told me about his flair for Mathematics, his outstanding credentials and Honours in Mathematics graduation, and how he renounced it all when he was invited to the Rashtrapati Bhavan once to play the guitar at a concert performance.

I am not certain the Rashtrapati Bhavan story was true. But he had put it on his CV. So, it must have been.

"Because you only live once," he kept telling me through this rejuvenation break.

"And what came of your performance at the Rashtrapati Bhavan?" I asked him.

"The President patted my back," he replied.

"Is that on your CV too?" I meant for it to be a joke, but he said yes, it was indeed on his CV and he would use it as leverage to get himself a fine job during Placement Week.

"Where is it that you'd like a job?" I asked.

He mulled over the question as we walked back to the institute; pensive, hands in pockets. "Well, there is a lot of time to that. Let us talk about it then."

We stopped outside the college gate. Govind's tea stall was active and running as always. Our go-to spot to recollect our thoughts in between lectures, Govind's tea tickled our nervous system like nothing else.

"Two, please." I placed a fiver on his table.

"Exams coming up?" Govind was always privy to the latest on campus.

"Terrible times ahead," I said as I watched him expertly toss a stream of tea from his pan into two plastic cups.

Suddenly, he put the pan down and pulled our palms forward, boring his eyes into them. "You won't have a good start. Early setbacks will make you resilient. Only to show that you will emerge as true champions."

Aryan saw me beaming with hope, then shot it down with a sane demand. "Govind, be more specific. Even my grandmother has told me this often."

"You are going to be ashamed of your first trimester results," he said plain-facedly.

Angrily we slammed our cups on his table, but he was undeterred. "So what, boys? Think of the end game. Your failure will only toughen you for the big fight. Both of you will walk away with the fattest pay cheques next year."

"Are you sure?" we asked him.

"Yes. Now," he slowly came to the matter of importance. "I charge hundred rupees for reading each palm. If my prediction comes true, of course. So I will wait for your trimester results and you can then pay me in cash. If in the meantime you'd like to refer equally anxious friends to me, I will be happy to quell their fears."

We returned to the library with vengeance on our minds. "There is no way on earth I will let Govind's prediction come true. Why, his cheek!"

"But he has also predicted fat pay cheques, remember?"

"Yeah, I take exception to the first half of his foretelling," I clarified. "Come on, now. Open that goddamn Economics book and shower me with your pearls of knowledge."

Alas! We had forgotten EVERYTHING. "How did this happen, I wonder?" I asked. "Does the rejuvenation break work only in Delhi's frigid climate?"

"Our minds are just very tired," he tried to explain, but his tone of conviction had significantly dwindled. "Let us take this up tomorrow morning. A fresh start."

"I don't want to trust you any more," I said, then added: "But what choice have I got tonight? Good night. I am going home."

"No, wait," he stopped me. "Let us go check on the others. Half the battle is won if we know that our friends are as screwed as we are."

"Really? Now that is your fallback?"

I was not sold on the trick but I tagged along anyway. The gang was still studying, they had clearly not taken a break – I could tell from their weary eyes, and when we stopped by their desk, their annoyance at being interrupted knew no bounds.

"How does it look?" Aryan asked them.

We had hoped for adjectives that would fit us in the same category of unpreparedness as us. But they told us things were going great and they had been cruising along and that Economics was not as difficult as some people made it out to be. Aryan and I exchanged looks of fatigue.

"Where is Sameer?" Vandana asked. "He is the Economics guru in our group. Maybe he can help you both."

"Overnight at Soha's house," Aryan told us.

"Oh yes, she had come purring to him in class," Vandana remembered. "About how she had not studied a single word all these weeks. He offered to spend some time with her."

"And hey, presto!" Aryan clapped his hands. "He reached her Worli residence to give her classes. If you know what I mean."

"Come on, maybe they actually *are* studying," she argued.

"Sure. But let me tell you he shaved thrice today," said Aryan. "This would be funny but I am not joking. Yes, he returned to the hostel after lunch and shaved one more time. I know because I saw his stubble left unrinsed in the sink when I went to my room in the evening. And I had already cleaned up twice after him in the morning."

"Too much information," Naina said with a cringe. "You need to go home, Aryan."

And go home, we did. But not before learning the hard way that just because you have a group of friends they are obliged to be as poorly prepared for a test as you are, and that failure is not a cigarette, a drag of which is equally shared between friends.

The next morning we woke up late, ruminated over what we could have done better, and then secured whatever peace of mind we could by re-reading all fourteen chapters, then memorising them by writing them in our scrapbooks, then debunking the stupid plan of division of labour that Aryan had brought to the table the previous night. When the day drew to a close, we shut our books and took a deep breath.

"How does it feel?" he asked.

"I remember some," I said. "I still forget some."

With his hands folded at the back of his head, he blew a soft whistle. "That is not a problem at all."

"I am sure you will elaborate," I said. "As always."

He sat up straight, beaming with excitement. "Look. My history teacher once told me the trick to writing long subjective answers in a paper. Look at the question and ask yourself: *Can I write something on this at least? Something?* Then, write *something* with a very impressive beginning and a mind-blowing ending. Look up some Economics quotes, for example."

"Quotes?"

"Or some fancy generic lines," he clucked his tongue irritably. *Why does this idiot have to be spoon-fed everything?* "The economy is on a boom. Market prices are sensitive. Read the offer document carefully before investing, whatever, man! And if you can use some diagrams to support your *something*, it is an extra win!"

"How much did you score in History?" I asked.

He burst out laughing. "Forget the past. Think about tomorrow. Trust me!"

10

The morning after the last exam filled us with a strange sense of lightness. The sunlight felt special; I had to shield my eyes from its splendour the first few seconds I stepped out. The sleeping bags we had brought to the library for an entire week were done away with. The toothpaste and toiletries had returned to our hostel rooms along with us. After a fresh shave and a shower, we gathered on the road outside to determine how to make the best of this newfound, if temporary, freedom.

"I know!" Swapnil snapped a finger before leading us stationward.

The travel agent's office off the station road was a decrepit, bonsai establishment with many betel stains and zero ventilation. Inside it were three pieces of furniture and an air that carried the combined fragrances of incense, betel paste and an expensive perfume that had been worn by the agency's owner Kamlesh Shah.

"So, where would you like to go?" he settled in his chair after taking a long phone call. "Switzerland, America, South Africa?"

We looked at him with wonder and shame. "Do you organise anything closer? Like, Mahabaleshwar?"

His passion for this discussion dropped like mercury in a thermometer. "You need an agent to take you to Mahabaleshwar? Well, ok." Reluctantly he pulled out some brochures. "Read them. The prices are all listed. I can get you a package if you guys are also looking for cheap eats there."

A holiday out of town and away from the rigmarole of college felt inviting. And also too good to be true, because when we reached campus holding Kamlesh Shah's brochures, the girls were waiting for us in the lobby, drawing our attention to a letter pinned to the noticeboard.

ATTENTION FIRST-YEAR FULL-TIME MBA STUDENTS: Reckitt &Coleman COMING TO THE CAMPUS FOR SUMMER PLACEMENTS TOMORROW. THOSE INTERESTED SUBMIT A HARD COPY OF YOUR BIODATA IN THE PLACEMENT OFFICE LATEST BY 4 PM TODAY.

"There goes the vacation!" I slumped into a chair with a sigh. "After all that hard work all week."

"Seriously?" Vandana looked at me. "Hard work, and you? Quite a drama queen, you are."

"And the trip is not cancelled, ok?" Swapnil assured me. "It is just delayed. Moreover, if we went after our summer placements, we'd have double cause to celebrate."

And thus we were back in the library for one more dreary afternoon, writing up biodatas with exaggerated achievements and fabricated experiences. Of one thing I was certain: if I did not land a job at the end of an MBA, I could surely start a business of writing fancy biodatas for young wastrels like me.

In the early evening when we had only barely finished lying through our teeth on the CVs, Sameer came bounding into the room like a child that had just witnessed a trapeze act.

"Guys, guess what!" he beamed. "Soha just called and…"

"Soha calling up must be a reason for you to cheer, Sameer…" I began.

"Cut it out jackass," Sameer said, visibly annoyed. "She called to inform us that she has five complimentary couple passes for Velocity tonight!"

"What's that?" Swapnil asked coldly.

"It's the coolest disc in Mumbai. The who's who of the tinsel town comes there."

"Well, I guess you can count me out, chum! I am really not in the mood tonight. I'd rather stay in college and look up some stuff for the interview tomorrow." Swapnil said.

"Me too! I think I'd rather catch up tonight on some sleep," concurred Aryan, "look at me! I look like a zombie!"

"And what about you?" Sameer looked at me.

"I don't mind coming," I said, "but I don't have a partner. Who do I dance with?"

"That's not a problem. You have more than two hours to look for one. So I'll see you at nine."

I looked up at Naina, the only girl at my table and the only girl as far as my eyes could take me that I'd have felt comfortable asking to accompany me to a dance.

"Don't look at me," she said, reading my mind.

"I thought you had promised to be a friend through thick and thin," I said accusingly.

"Yeah, you are not dying, dude." She raised a finger to her lips to shut me up.

I walked around campus until I found Vandana, sitting calmly in the canteen and sipping on a hot cup of cocoa.

"How would you like to come along with me for a dance tonight?" I came straight to the point.

She cocked a brow at my abruptness. Placing the cup on the table, she asked. "Am I your Hobson's choice?"

"Second choice," I admitted. "Not going to lie. But a valuable one nonetheless."

"Who was the first choice?"

"Naina." I considered her reaction.

An *I knew it* rather than a *How could you?* "Have you ever seen me dance, Nakul?"

"You haven't seen me dance, either," I winked. "Hey look, we don't *have* to go dance there. We can just take to the couch, get some drinks, order some finger food, check out any celebrities who might rock up there."

"Who else is coming?" she asked.

"Sameer and Soha," I said. "Wow, that's some thorough interrogation you are doing, aren't you?"

She laughed. "It does not matter. Ok, Nakul. I will come. What time do we go?"

"I have no clothes to wear!" Sameer cried out in despair, pointing me towards a wardrobe overloaded with shirts of every colour in the spectrum and a dozen pairs of pants in corduroy, denim, and gaberdine.

"I see what you are saying," I said dryly, looking around at the shirts he had flung onto his bed in search of the perfect one. "But why do you care? You are getting your clothes off at the end of the dance anyway, aren't you?"

He wagged a finger before my eyes. "No dirty jokes about Soha, get it?"

Laughter escaped my tightened lips despite my best attempt at showing restraint. "Surely you don't get it on with your clothes on. Here, try this one."

He examined with unhappiness a dandy green shirt I had flicked at him from the wreckage that lay on his bed. "No, it is not bright enough."

Ah, now I understood. Sameer needed gold. I scoured his shirts again before finally showing him a short kurta with so much studding at its seams it would not clear the metal detector at an airport's security gates.

"Ok, this will have to do." He sprayed five rounds of deodorant on his bare torso before bringing it up.

"Can we go now?" I asked finally, looking at my watch.

He looked at himself in the mirror, then at me – with a circumspect gaze. "How do I look?"

"Adonis!" I sprang to my feet and pushed him out the door.

The disc was a long hour away from the hostel. Sameer vetoed the train option on this night because he could not risk contaminating his carefully deodorised skin with the slightest hint of perspiration. He ordered us a cool cab after repeatedly assuring me he would singlehandedly foot the bill. On the way, he asked me if he should tell Soha he loves her.

"Wait," I interrupted him. "You haven't told her yet?"

"It is implicit," he explained.

The last time I had tried offering him advice on the matter, he had taken offence. Because I had limited to no patience to deal with a friend's emotional outburst again, I just shrugged and told him he should follow his heart.

What I had forgotten to add was he should follow his heart only as long as he stayed sober, for by the time we met Soha and Vandana at the entrance of Velocity, he was already two beers down and emotionally overcharged.

"You look very pretty," he told Soha who was dressed in a turquoise off-shoulder dress with a Coach purse to boot.

"Aw, thank you!" She blew a generic-as-fuck kiss in the air inhabited by him at the moment, and he took it as a sign of romantic development.

"Shall we go?" he offered her his arm, squarely ignoring the presence of Vandana who had painstakingly dressed up in a newly acquired pair of stonewashed Levi's denim and a beige top from Marks & Spencer.

"Sameer is blind," I said, offering Vandana a hug. "But you look gorgeous too."

She dismissed my explanation with a wave. "Oh, that was expected of him. I did not mind it at all. Thanks for the compliment anyway."

We followed the other couple towards the dance floor, a space enough to accommodate three hundred people. Halogen lights of various colours throbbed overhead. Loud music blared from the DJ's console, invigorating the dancing enthusiasts and nauseating novices like me. The DJ presented an assortment of music ranging from contemporary rock to hip-hop and depending on the speed of the number he either gyrated left to right or bounced in his position like a yoyo. Sameer and Soha were already lost in one another's arms on the dance floor, and if their body language was anything to go by, he did not need to spell out to her that he was in love with her. Unless, of course, she was fishing for the exact words so she could draw out a contract.

Off the dance floor, several people were sprawled on couches with their cigarettes and drinks, taking breaks from an intense dance session or having simply decided to steer clear of any aerobics for the evening.

"I must admit I have two left feet," I said to Vandana after realising the anxiety of standing on a laser-infused dance floor was too much for me to bear. "Sorry, I should have told you earlier."

She threw her hands up in the air in mock exasperation. "Great, I can go home now!"

"Oh no, please don't," I pleaded. "I am feeling terrible. Come, let us dance."

She placed her hands on my shoulders. "Chill. I have no problem if we just sat and talked. But I am curious – why are you here if you did not want to dance?"

I ran a hand in a circle overhead. "The vibe. I had heard about the place's vibe. But now I think I have another reason too."

I motioned towards Sameer, who had now attained the highest level of acceptable inebriation before the black-clothed bouncers marched up and whisked him away. He had taken off his shirt and wrapped it around his waist. His vest was not only significantly less glittery than his shirt but was also poked with holes as big as the ones in a block of Swiss Cheese.

"Oh, my God!" Vandana gasped.

"Exactly," I said. "I need to take that creature home once he is done with his antics."

Soha seemed not in the least perturbed by the antics. She danced like there was no tomorrow, in or out of Sameer's locked embrace. When she swayed away from him and lost herself in the crowd on the floor – presumably because she had noticed the Swiss Cheese punctures in his Lux Cozi – he remembered my existence and came prancing to me.

"Brother!" He threw his arms around me. The sweat on his arms stuck to my cheeks like glue. "Thanks for coming. Oh, hi Naina!"

"Vandana."

"Vandana!" He hugged her too. "Your moral support matters. I want you to know."

She looked at us, confused. "Moral support?"

"Tell her, ok?" Sameer looked at me. "I need to get back out there before the opportunity is lost. And listen, Nakul?"

"Yeah?"

"I am not in the best of my senses," he laughed. "If you see me do anything silly, just snap your finger like this." He snapped his fingers to demonstrate.

"Brilliant plan," I said, snapping my finger a few times. But he was gone already, back into the sea of people in search of his lady love.

Vandana turned to me again. "Moral support?" He is going to tell her" I said. Noting disapproval in her scowl, I asked. "You don't think it is a great idea, do you?"

"I think it is a great idea I don't make it my business," she shrugged. "Hey listen, let's get something to eat?"

I considered Sameer for a moment; he had found Soha again. The music was intense, she was keeping him busy, and he was still stable on his feet. What was the worst that could happen? "Yeah, let's get some food."

We went up to the bartender and ordered two overpriced burgers that we carried to one of the couches at the far back.

"I can't believe this thing costs a hundred bucks," she spoke amidst mouthfuls. "They should see the beauties served at the little eateries on Nainital's Mall Road. Far cheaper and far better."

I watched her, carefully pushing back the little slices of tomato that escaped her bun. "You miss home a lot, don't you?"

"Don't we all?" she asked me. "Yes, I miss it a lot. Every waking moment. I just yearn to go back home. What about you?"

I pursed my lips in thoughtful consideration. "I can't say I miss it as much as I thought I would. I mean yes, sure. Being with family is a great feeling. But having been able to find me a family away from home is very special too."

"Family away from home?" she asked unsurely. "Who do you mean?"

"Why, all of you, of course, Vandana!" I exclaimed. "You, Naina, these boys that hang out with us – as silly as their antics are. I love you all!"

She ran a tongue over the roof of her mouth to keep from smiling. "Sure."

"Sure? That's all you have got?" I was almost offended by the callousness in her response.

"It never replaces one's actual family, this – this structure," she raised her hands to explain. "Don't get me wrong. I love you too just as much. But, no. You are not family. You are all going away in two years. Family doesn't go anywhere. Family stays."

I shook my head with displeasure. "So, you have decided it's all quits once we walk out of that convocation ceremony."

"Prove me wrong when the day comes," she challenged me. "Come on, Nakul. I have been there. At that stage when I felt it all lasts forever. Guess what? It does not."

I stopped to read the pain in her allegation. "Is there something you want to talk about?"

"There is nothing to talk about," she answered. "Yes, there was someone I studied with. Someone who gave me the Forever Spiel. That flight got grounded before it could even take off. I don't mind it, really. I am over it myself. And I think you should brace yourself too. Just a bit of friendly advice."

"What do I need to brace myself against?" I asked, perplexed.

She cocked her head sideward in a smile. "Lots happening over coffee lately, eh?"

"Naina?" I asked with a frown.

"We have roommate updates every night," she said with a wink.

"And?"

"And, nothing," she said. "I just thought I will let you know Naina is – how do I put it now – a very practical person. Not one to get swayed by…"

"I am going to have to stop you there, girl,' I said with a laugh. 'You are getting it all wrong. There is nothing on between me and your roommate."

"I know there is not," she agreed. "As I said, she is a very practical person. Does not easily give in to emotional vulnerability."

"As am I," I insisted. "She is just a very dear friend. I don't know what has given you the impression there is anything else to it. Wait. Has she said something?"

"Oh no, she has not!" She widened her eyes as she attempted a clarification. "She has only the nicest things to say about you. She speaks fondly of you. Of a dear friend she has found in you, and all that. You may just want to keep your own emotions in check, that is all."

"They are in check,' I said flatly. 'Because she is just a friend. Like you all are."

"I could be reading it wrong, then,' she said. 'You seem to care for her a lot more than you'd care for a friend. Special friend, maybe? That's even trickier. What future exists for a relationship between *special friends* that are nothing more? That road ends soon, my dear."

"Let's agree to disagree, then," I said. "I will come knocking at your door soon after we have graduated. Just a heads up."

She turned over her shoulder. Sameer's shirt was back on. He was now stumbling as he danced. Soha had him by the waist as they swayed to a mellow number that the DJ had used to lure the dancers into a tempered-down tango. When we returned to the dance floor, she let go of him, allowing him to drop on the floor like a sack of rice.

"Guys, guess what! Sameer just proposed to me!"

He sat on the floor, gazing at us with dreamy eyes. "I did, didn't I? Did she say yes?"

We looked at Soha for an answer. "Hmm, I don't know. I need to test the waters before I jump in."

My blood was now boiling over. "That is an actual person you are talking about. It is a yes or a no. How hard can it be?"

Vandana clutched at my hand. "No overstepping," she whispered.

Soha stepped up to me, high-nosed, and scoffed at my demand. "If you think testing the waters is asking for too much, you go and say yes to him. You two will make a fine pair too."

Saying so, she stomped off towards the washroom. We lingered on for a while until Sameer was at least willing to clamber up on his feet. I then threw one of his arms around my shoulder and hailed a cool cab (after securing his wallet in my possession). Vandana rode along with us because Soha wanted to continue partying – with or without us. Half an hour into the drive, Sameer's phone came alive with a text message.

He was knocked out for the night. I slid the phone out of his shirt pocket. "One unread message: Soha."

"Put it back," Vandana admonished me. "Have some manners!"

I put it back in his pocket and then drew it out again. "I am pathetic, I know. I just have to see this."

"Nakul! No!"

But the horses had bolted. I was now too invested in Sameer's private matters to let go. "Sorry. Kill me later. I have to read this."

Hey Sam, I pondered a lot about what you said last night. I must say it's too early for me to commit, but we can make a start. Lotsa love…

With the elegance and charm of a sorceress, she drew him into a whirlpool of hopes and fanciful dreams, and in return rode on arguably the most fun-filled moments of her life. He sat extra hours and taught her lessons done in classes that she missed due to party hangovers the previous night. He finished her pending assignments when she could not keep extra hours in college on account of her countless social obligations. He dropped her home every evening after classes and then returned to the hostel all alone in a rickshaw so he could spend an extra hour with her. And of course, there were those frequent dinner treats that kept happening at regular intervals. Besotted by the magic of her doe-like eyes and sugary voice, his emotions trumped sanity and logic.

But, "No overstepping," they kept reminding me.

That left us with little choice but to wait and watch before the curtains rose over this whirlwind courtship.

12

Leaving aside certain landmark events like my laptop crashing after I left it out in the rain, borrowing my first book from the library which I never read, and Soha finally accepting Sameer's proposal, little significance could be attached to the period between the end of our first trimester exams and our Diwali break. This time passed soon, but the break passed by even sooner. And before we could realise it, we were back in Mumbai after a short junket home for the second round of infliction by the rigour of nine new subjects. The vacation did give us respite from the boring lectures, the penalties for late submission of huge assignments, and the forgettable memories of preparing for the trimester exams. But at the same time, it made us miss the lighter moments spent on campus, our jamming sessions in the hostel corridor, and the crass jokes we cut at Govind's tea stall. It made us miss the mock "group discussions" we had on the terrace of our hostel through starry nights.

Rigour and stress had an interesting way of greeting us after the leisure time we spent at home. The first message that flashed on the notice board at the entrance was: KIND ATTENTION FIRST-YEAR STUDENTS: RESULTS OF THE FIRST TRIMESTER EXAMINATIONS OUT. RESULTS ON DISPLAY AT 2 PM.

"Why did they have to announce this at 10 AM itself?" I wailed.

For the first time since I had known him, Aryan's face turned white with horror. "I know. Sadists! This is four hours of unnecessary death by anxiety."

"I am failing at least one subject," I said. "What about you?"

That awkward moment when you invite a friend to partake in your grief by telling you he is in the same cesspool as you are, but he flatly refuses to. "I won't fail. I was not that bad."

I skipped class and deposited myself outside the secretary's office until the door opened. My gut churned. My limbs froze. My eyes burnt with a raging fever. I was less consumed by the worry of my future than I was about being left behind in my group of friends. As the door to the secretary's office opened, my worst fears came true. But even before the report card was handed to me, I received from Naina a printout containing assignments on Corporate Strategy that were due the following week.

"Four caselets," she stated as she casually strode into the secretary's office and asked for her report card. "Naina Rai."

The assistant behind the glass façade slipped it out through an opening at the bottom. "Well done!" she said, reading the score on the certificate.

"Thanks!" Naina smiled back before turning to me. 'Get yours. I am waiting outside.'

I picked up my mark sheet and ran out of the wretched room with my eyes closed. "Read it out for me," I handed it to her.

She read it and drew a long sigh. "Nakul."

My heart sank as I snatched the mark sheet from her, at which she laughed and placed her head on my shoulder. "Look at you! You have passed!"

"I have?" I took a close look at the print for the first time. My heart did a little dance on seeing PASS written at the header. "Naina! This is all thanks to you!"

"Say no more," she patted me as I breathed easy for the first time since that morning. But what she asked me next knocked the wind out of my sails once again. "What is your GPA?"

This was the first time I had heard of a beast called Grade Point Average. The academic system's concept of sarcasm as it assigned you a number to denote how superior or inferior to your colleagues you had proven yourself to be.

I read out the number with a quiver in my voice. "2.86 on 4. What the hell does this mean?"

She recoiled in horror on hearing the figure. Like it was a contagion that could pass on by being uttered. The laughing head that had been placed on my shoulder was now back where it belonged. Instead, her hand rubbed my back in solace. "Come, let's get some tea."

"No, I don't want tea," I stood my ground like a child who had been denied a toy at the dollar store. "What does 2.86 mean – is it good or bad? Or, very bad? How much have you got?"

She tried scampering away but I grabbed her report card and had a look anyway. "3.25. That seems a lot higher."

"Let's get that tea now," she said again, but I had now hunted down everyone else's report cards. Sameer had 3.2. Vandana had 3.44. Swapnil had – oh my dear God, Swapnil had topped the batch with a staggering 3.81. I suddenly didn't care about having passed any more. I wanted ONE person who had a 2.86 or below. Once again, it was Aryan I found myself being able to depend on as I found him sitting in a corner of the quad, moping quietly and pensively even as he pretended to play it cool by chewing on Happydent.

"How much?" I asked hopefully.

He knew why I was asking him. To seek succour in his failures. He did not mind my selfishness. "2.75."

I must have been the most horrid friend one could have hoped for. But I found it humanly impossible to conceal my relief even as I patted him comfortingly. "Never mind. There is always another time."

"I just wonder what went wrong this time," he scratched his scraggly beard pensively.

"It could have something to do with your History teacher's advice," I considered. "And that strategy of drawing graphs with multi-coloured sketch pens."

At this, he sprang up and held me by my shoulders. "Worry not, brother! Let us not lose hope. We have hit rock bottom this time only because from this point we can just get a lot better."

I scoffed at his dogged pursuit of motivating me. "Let us go pay Govind first. We owe him hundred rupees because he had prophesied our fate. Once we are done with him, let us find a way to cure your extreme optimism."

At Govind's, we dispensed the said fee and sought solace in his repeated reassurance that we were still walking home with the best salaries in the batch. Notwithstanding his encouragement, Nilesh, who had eavesdropped on the entire conversation while munching on bread pakoras, laughed out loud at Govind's absurd claim.

"Nakul will get the best salary? Govind, you crack me up!"

I drew a sharp breath to deal with having to put up with Nilesh until we were done drinking our tea. Nilesh was the mythological *Garuda* of our batch. He only presented himself to the world when he felt the urge to be the bearer of bad news.

Hey class. We now have two days less to deliver the assignment to Prof. Biswas.

Hi class. The canteen prices will be up 10% starting next month.

Hi Nakul. I heard you scored a 2.86? Did you know Professor Wankhede reckons no one in the history of this institute has scored as low as 2.86?

"Aryan, meet Nilesh," I offered. "If you haven't already. He fills us in with some extremely interesting information. For example, he just followed me to the washroom a few minutes back only to tell me I have broken the record of scoring the lowest GPA in the history of this institute. Isn't he resourceful, Aryan?"

"Resourceful," Aryan nodded. "But I can't say much about his accuracy. Hi Nilesh, I am Aryan. I scored 2.75."

Nilesh needed his hands to be sufficiently dramatic. So he placed the plate of bread pakoras on Govind's stall, put his hands to his face like a beauty queen who had unexpectedly been crowned and screamed. "2.75? Why so less?"

Aryan noticed my irresistible urge to slap the living daylights out of Nilesh. With a blink, he told me to rein in my emotions. "Govind here is a fine astrologer. He told me that numerology told him the number 2.75 would bring with it unprecedented good luck for Aryan Nair."

Nilesh grumpily stuffed the rest of the pakora in his mouth and walked off in a huff. "I was just trying to be friends. You didn't have to be nasty."

I looked at Aryan with a shrug and disgust. "What sort of people are we surrounded by?"

"Let us go to the beach," he said. "Seagulls are a lot better than humans."

"Are there seagulls in Bombay?"

"Who knows," he shrugged. "This day is full of surprises."

We took to our usual spot by the beach. Felt the soft, comforting sand of the shore. The rains had long receded and had sent in a cool change from the sweltering humidity we had seen all year. Locals had thronged the *chowpatty* once again. Like the Twelve Apostles lining the coastline of the Pacific, couples had placed themselves at equidistant spots along the low tide. Some held hands, others locked arms, and a few that were oblivious to the prying eye of the average voyeur – locked lips. Over the horizon, the moon had barely begun to rise; a white circular ball hung over the edge of the water and cast over it a sliver of white light.

"Do you think grades are a selection criterion during Placement?" I asked. I knew the answer to the question. But hearing a 'No' was a necessary panacea to the mental stress that was now building up close to the end of the first year.

"Not at all." Aryan obliged me with the response I was seeking. 'They look at all-round development.'

"That is nice to hear," I said, closing my eyes.

"We need to think beyond textbooks," he said. "Do you know what I mean?"

"No, I do not," I said. "But I won't stop you today. Anything you recommend will do as long as it makes me feel better."

"We need to read a lot more," he continued, brimming with sagely confidence. "Let us start reading a magazine every night in the library. Marketing, Finance, Operations – whatever we feel like. But let us read one magazine every day."

"One magazine every day," I repeated.

"And the newspapers," he added.

"Newspapers."

"And let us participate in every B-school fest that comes our way," he said. "We are going to have loads of them in the second year. Let us team up and win some awards, man. See where these accolades take us."

I nodded. "We should go back right now, Aryan. Right now. To the library. I want to pick up that magazine at this very moment and change the course of my future. Enough is enough. Are you listening?"

He was not. He looked straight into the distance, in the direction of the couples that stood nearly motionless against the gentle splashing of waves at their feet. "Do you see what I see?"

I followed his vision to a specific couple right in our line of sight. Caring two hoots about the universe, they were now engaged in a passionate kiss that lasted long enough for us to set a timer on. "So? What are you Aryan, a twelve-year-old?"

"Shut up," he taunted me. "You are blind. That guy is our senior, Sambhav."

"I am not blind," I argued. "You are an eagle. How can you see so clearly in the dark?"

He shook his head firmly. "I just know it is him. But that's not what is bothering me."

"Then what is?" I asked, now confused as well as intrigued.

"Who is the girl with him?" he asked.

I squinted my eyes as I exerted myself to look at them closely. "Someone."

"Not just someone," he said irritably. "I am going to go find out."

"By going up to them and saying hello?"

"I might just go ask them the time," he had now started to walk.

I tailed him with a fervent request for him to stop. "That is just preposterous. Don't!"

"You stay back if you don't want to," he quickened his pace. "Nakul, I am telling you. She is…"

"Soha." I stopped in my tracks. We were ten feet away. But I did not need to go any closer to confirm my fear. The silhouette was unmistakably hers – wrapped around Sambhav's arms, unaware of our prying eyes trained on them.

I pulled out my phone and furiously dialled a number. "Hello, Sameer? You are not going to believe what I just saw."

13

Naina had a long list of conditions when it came to deciding a place to eat. I first realised it when I asked her where she would like to be treated for helping me in Financial Management. I had to my surprise, passed with a decent B+ in the subject, and now dutifully agreed to fulfil my promise.

"Let's see," she began, "I am mildly hungry, but not ravenous. So do you have any place in mind?"

"Sukh Sagar?" I asked.

"No way!" she cried. "The food's too oily there."

"Bistro's?" I suggested.

"That's only a kebab corner," she complained, "I don't think they serve coffee there, do they? A treat isn't complete without a nice hot cup of coffee!"

"Café Coffee Day?"

"The music is so loud there my head hurts!"

We finally went to Cuppa Café, where she ordered an Espresso Americano (without sugar), a Manchurian Roll, and a handful of tissues. I watched in astonishment as she picked each tissue one by one and caressingly soaked out all the possible oil from the roll till it was reduced to the look of a dry twig.

"Why the big fuss about the calories?" I asked. "You are in good shape!"

"I am?" she asked, beaming with sudden joy.

"Of course," I said, "even round is a shape!" and burst out laughing until I saw her cringe. "Sorry. Was I being overfamiliar?"

"No, you were just belting out an old joke," she retorted. "I expected better from you."

"But seriously," I changed track. "You don't need to worry about the extra oil."

"Yeah, but if I don't do this," she said, pointing towards the oil-soaked handful of tissues, "it could cause a lot of damage. Moreover, I hardly engage in any physical activity. I am too lazy for that!"

The chilly cheese croissant suddenly lost its flavour. I felt my double chin trouble my conscience again. Alright, so I jogged every morning like a maniac. But my fondness for cheese and chocolates had manifested itself in creating their permanent abodes in and around my face and chin. Besides, I never wiped my food with tissues.

"So, what have you decided about summers?" she asked.

"What about them?" I asked, putting my food away. If the topic of calories was not enough to kill my appetite, the top-up with the S-word surely did. "Summers? I will just," unsure of how to put it, I said, "go with the flow."

"What flow?" she tested me. "The Marketing flow? The Finance flow? The HR or Operations flow? Do you know what flow?"

"Do you have to sermonise?" I asked irritably. "Especially when you are right?"

"Nakul!" she rolled her eyes in disbelief. "Twenty-three students from our batch have already got placed. You need to buck up!"

"Twenty-three," I pondered. "That includes you, doesn't it?"

"I didn't want to bring that up, but yes," she said. "Includes me. And this list must include you very soon."

"We have only just scraped through our exams," I moaned.

"Only just?" she asked. "It's been two months. You look like you are on a picnic."

"Alright, alright," I resigned. "So I need to think about it. I will start. Tonight, right after dinner, ok? Let me identify a list of Marketing jobs."

She continued staring at me, a hint of a smile along with some suspicion reaching her eyes. "I told you I will do it," I said. "Now can we discuss something else at least while eating?"

She relented. "Ok, tell me. How is Sameer taking the news about Soha and what you saw on the beach?"

"He is hardly taking it well," I spoke sadly. "Maybe he was better off not hearing it from us."

"What nonsense!" she grunted. "You did the right thing. He would have found out one way or the other."

"Soha went apologising to him once he found out what she was up to," I said. "*Just a silly mistake*, apparently."

"Rubbish." Her tone curdled with disgust. "It's just ridiculous to imagine you can place your trust in anyone."

I took a minute or two to respond. "It'll never be difficult for you to trust me," I said, placing my hand in hers, "I don't know about anyone else."

She laughed a little. "I trust you," she said, patting me on the shoulder, "I really do. You are a great friend."

"It's mutual," I said, "it's in fact your greatness that percolates down to me when I am in your company."

She laughed louder this time. "You sure are a great flatterer, aren't you?"

I was not flattering her. I meant in complete earnestness every word that I said. But I don't think I could ever articulate to her in clear terms what I meant.

14

Trimesters came and went, but the innate laziness took its own time to cease. Sub-three grades were now a routine event. Aryan and I had become immune to any kind of shock that would emanate therefrom. We, in fact, formed a small club of sub-three graders who treated ourselves to mini meals at McDonald's every time our results were out. Together with friends, one can look for the funniest of reasons to celebrate. If nothing else, it helps relieve you of the guilt of having fallen short of achieving something significant. In our case, our report cards showed us a different perspective: each time we were getting closer to becoming full-fledged MBAs.

My single biggest achievement in the first year was my summer placement with a reputed pharmaceutical company in Mumbai. A semi-crumpled shirt and zilch knowledge of the pharma sector notwithstanding, I had managed to pull this one off and was pretty satisfied with myself. It did not matter much that Nilesh, like the ever-dependable *Garuda* flew up to me and told me the real reason I had got placed.

"Because there were only twenty students left," he said. "Everyone else was already placed. And as a responsible member of the Students' Council, I got some previously placed guys to sit with you in that room and tank their performance in the Group Discussion."

I told him I was forever grateful to him and that I would find a suitable time to repay him in full someday; maybe I could offer to wash his feet until such time?

"We are pleased to have you for our summer training programme," the marketing head of the company had told me as I shook hands with him. "We expect you now to live up to our expectations in terms of your effort, and we in turn promise you a rewarding experience."

I felt tempted to ask him what exactly their expectations were from a naïve gullible trainee, but thank God for small mercies that I did not. "Thank you, Sir, it will be a pleasure to work with you."

The words "pleasure" and "work" did sound paradoxical to me, but now that I had spoken them with such flourish, I thought it wise to pull up my socks in any case. I marched to the library with gusto and got myself two books issued on pharmaceutical marketing.

"You want both together?" the Librarian asked me at the counter.

"Yes, I do, can't I…?" I asked.

He grinned. "Of course, you can! You'll have to return both in ten days."

"I know that," I said, "I'll be done with both within four days."

He looked at me in mock admiration and then continued. "Have you read "The Blue Ocean Strategy', by the way?"

"No, I haven't. What about it?"

"You got that book issued before Diwali, in case you do not remember! The return of that book is about eighty-one days overdue. According to the late fee rule of two rupees per day, you are one hundred and sixty-two rupees in debt."

I flushed in embarrassment and my mind raced back in time, trying to recall when I ever laid my hands on a book by that name. It later transpired that borrowing this book was a consequence of the discussion Aryan and I had on the beach the other evening. Aryan had said in his trademark style, *"Kuch kar dikhaayenge!"* (We will show our worth to the world!) and that had given me a tremendous but temporary boost, and subsequently a sudden urge to get hold of the book. The idea of reading the book was to get some useful ideas for the Corporate Strategy exam in the second trimester, but it remained just an idea at the end of the day.

The third trimester was a three-month-long party interjected with a spate of assignments. But these submissions and exams did not seem to affect us much any longer in terms of mental pressure. Maybe we had got used to the rigmarole. Maybe the company of good friends served as an energiser that pulled us out of the jaws of frustration each time we were cowed down by the pressure of academics and placements. Partying, bantering around on campus, and exploring parts of the city had become the order of the day. Even as we entered the two months of summer training, on-site career counsellors started paying occasional visits to give us career tips, I busied myself carving little moments from every day that would adorn my 'Dear Diary' pages. Friends became a necessity, an addiction I found indispensable. Swapnil and Sameer were my regular saviours during the exams. Swapnil's perfection in imbibing and recapitulating every word and syllable discussed by the faculty in the classroom, combined with Sameer's insatiable quest to devour all the management journals and e-manuals under the sun, made it fairly easy for me to learn enough to not fail my exams.

Sameer never mentioned Soha again after the beach episode. We gladly laid the matter to rest too. We were vaguely aware of one more time they had met after the incident, when Soha had tried to play around with the story, giving some hogwash that Sambhav had played angel to her during her past phase of distress, and that she was just being nice to him in return. She accused Aryan and me of having blown the story out of proportion. But this time, wisdom outplayed Sameer's emotions. Following that incident, however, he became a changed person. He tended to keep a little aloof. Whether it was because he had developed a general distrust towards everyone around, or whether it was a comeuppance he was serving upon himself for having fallen for a girl who changed her loyalties as per her need of the hour, we didn't know.

Soha had, for her part, already begun to pay for her deeds. By the end of the first year, her tendencies had come to be understood and despised by one and all, and the number of people who had come to recognise her true colours had significantly risen. Perhaps one always must pay a heavy price for being opportunistic at the end of the day. Usually, my heart would be compelled to go out to her, because I do know the angst of feeling lonely in a crowd. The avoid-the-jerk vibe can be a killer. If only the human mind could foresee such alienation when they behaved as they did, friendship, goodwill and relationships would be much easier to sustain.

My distrust and disdain for Soha brought about an equivalent increase in fondness for Naina and Vandana. I could happily lose myself in their company, be totally and utterly myself with them – my unapologetic, unabashed self and I could still earn their love. Even so, I recognised the credit for the sustenance of these relationships went entirely to the girls. Vandana always made it a point to go and ask every single friend or acquaintance visible in every single corner of the campus if they would like to come along with her for dinner. Such was Vandana, who knew how to apportion her time for everyone who mattered to her. One could hardly ever complain about any inadequacy in the concern she showed for her friends. A night before our Corporate Finance exam when she sat explaining concepts to Aryan and me, it spoke volumes of her dedication. "You will not goddamn yawn or say that you are hungry until you have solved this one problem on your own," she admonished us with a tone of authority for the first time. The admonishment was well accepted, and that night was one of those rare nights when Aryan and I did not yawn any more till we were in the library under her watchful eyes.

Yet, inching above every friendship I had developed here was the equation I felt with Naina as my opinion of her meandered into the grey area that lay between friendship and something else that could never be named. Whenever I was questioned about it, I fought back the allegation with a strongly worded 'We are just friends' even if I knew that was reasonable but not quite entirely true. It hardly mattered, did it? Because I needed to give no explanation to her for anything. She never asked me for one.

15

Dilip Desai, or DD as I called him, was the only other guy from my college who interned with VRF Pharma. We did not get off to what we could call the most auspicious start to our summer training. Our otherwise ever-reliable BEST bus broke down minutes after it left the first stop from Vile Parle. My watch showed eight forty-five, which meant that we were going to be late to work on the very first day, which in turn meant a severe pounding from the boss.

"What do we do now?" I asked. "Go to the next stop?"

"Of course not," he replied. "It will take us forever to get there. And the morning traffic is anyway a killer. Let us just take the train."

I stalled and baulked, remembering my first – and very unpleasant – experience riding a Mumbai local. "What are our other alternatives?"

"Reaching office by lunchtime!" he hissed.

Getting smashed in a jam-packed local on a sultry May morning felt moderately more bearable than rocking up late to work on the first day and dealing with the wrath of the man who would be our reporting manager for the next eight weeks. "The train it is, then."

As we stood on the platform waiting for the next train, we cast nervous glances at our watches. "We have had it today," DD said. "Not reaching there before 10 AM."

I pictured us entering a long hall with scores of other trainees seated around a table. At the centre would be seated three forty-something grumpy executives, fuming at us, ready to hurl an array of unsavoury opinions on our lack of discipline and punctuality.

"Ours is a highly professional organisation that respects time. We would expect you to appreciate our values and learn to be a little more punctual than that," they would say. We would mumble our apologies and yet get judged by those steely eyes…

The train pulled to a halt at the platform, bringing me back to the moment. A year in Mumbai had toughened me. Therefore, while I was still not excited about sandwiching myself amidst sweat and stink, I knew better than to politely wait in line for my turn to get in. I brought out my inner Hulk and muscled my way through the crowd even as a much skinnier DD just slid into the compartment as a snake crawls into a hole. We stood by the window for as long as we rode, letting the warm wind fan the sweat beads on our foreheads. It was ten-thirty by the time we reached the VRF Pharma office – a tall glass building housed in a sprawling corporate complex next to the Lower Parel mills. The estate had lush green lawns and pretty fountains, but nary an employee was found spending leisure time in their comfort.

We ran up to the HR department on the second floor. HR was busy charting an employee engagement plan via tickets to a music festival when we interrupted them.

"We are looking for Avinash Jalan, please," we knocked on the wall partitioning their cubicle.

"Trainees?"

"Yes Sir," DD replied. "Sorry, we are late. Our bus broke down on the way."

"Oh no you are not," they laughed. "Avinash himself walked in ten minutes ago. If he gives you grief for being late, tell him we have told on him already."

They directed us to a cabin at the far end of the floor. Avinash Jalan was crouched in his chair, his eyes squinting hard at his laptop screen as he tried to concentrate on whatever it was he was doing. "Come in," he said without looking up, not aware we were already in and standing right over his head. "Be with you in a minute."

What he did not know was his screen was partly exposed to us. I saw he was on Mario Brothers, World 1-3. And the poor guy was not able to get past a wide cliff.

"Sir, use Ctrl+Alt together," I suggested, much to DD's chagrin. "It will give you extra speed."

Avinash looked up with a start and shut his laptop. "And you are?"

"Trainees, Sir," I said.

"Only first names, please," he insisted. "Welcome. I was waiting for you. What can I do for you?"

We stared at him, confused. *We* were supposed to tell *him?* "Just keen to get started, Avinash."

Heavily distraught by his video game having been disturbed, Avinash pinched his eyes. When he opened them again, we saw in them the burden of an entire universe, a reluctance to train his trainees, and an utter lack of motivation at being employed with VRF Pharma.

He threw his hands around in the air and stammered. "Yes. So what would you like to get started with? We do a lot of things here."

"We were hoping you'd have an assignment for us in mind," we told him.

He fingered his French beard as though it were a scratch card beneath which lay the magic answer. "Do you know much about Salesforce?"

"Vaguely," we replied. We knew nothing. But we wanted to sell ourselves a tad longer than what we were actually capable of.

"Our company has just started using Salesforce automation to analyse sales trends in our Cardiac Division for prescription drugs." Seeing us nod with vigour, he continued. "Why don't you go down to our reading hall and pick some manuals on Salesforce? Read up today. Let's get on the field tomorrow."

The library in the office had books on all topics under the sun, ranging from the literature on the pharmaceutical industry to gossip magazines of the glitterati. The comfy velvet sofas were a massive temptation to stretch and put me to sleep, especially after a good lunch, so in the initial days, I made a conscious effort to avoid the sofas and take an upright position on the straight chairs and the table. On the first day, we meticulously read and took down notes of whatever we found significant in the SFA manuals. We compared the pre and post-SFA implementation sales figures in the Cardiac Division and made notes of the difference SFA had made in the company's growth of sales. At the end of Day One, we felt we had conquered the world. We ran back to Jalan to tell him how proud he should be feeling of us.

"He is again not in his seat," DD hissed. "That's the fourth break I am seeing this chap take after lunch. Does he do anything at all?"

"Shh," I cautioned, "there are eagles in the air. Don't get us in trouble. And in any case, we should be happy; this indicates we can also take as many breaks as we want to!"

"No boss," DD protested, "I, for one, have not come here for a picnic. I have come here to do something worthwhile, and we had better get some good attention and guidance here."

This was the basic problem in working with overly sincere people. They would contradict you just when you would begin to hope there was room for some fun in work. Jalan returned after a good twenty minutes. We showed him our proposals and asked for his go-ahead.

He read them briefly before looking up with droopy eyes. "Yeah, it looks good. Come down tomorrow, and we shall decide how to begin."

After a harried first day at my first job ever, I committed a cardinal error of topping up my despair with a visit to the campus during the summer break. The college was deserted and empty, robbed of the usual din and chatter that usually gave it life. The seniors had graduated and moved on to their respective jobs. We had busied ourselves with our summers, and only a fraction of us had landed assignments in Mumbai. A vast majority had scored placements elsewhere, including Vandana and Aryan – who via frequent messages on MSN Chat - kept me abreast with how badly they were getting baked selling colas and chips on the scorching Delhi streets. Of the few that were in the city, even fewer chose to visit the institute after work. It was usually the closest bar or the cinemas, or for simpler choices – the hostel bed.

The following day Jalan asked us once again what we'd like to do. I was now convinced this was a trick question and I hence chose the most unsavoury answer which given a choice, I would not offer myself over my dead body. Especially in the middle of May.

"I'd like to get on the field."

"Great idea, said Jalan with such a lack of passion he could have very well been saying 'Today is Tuesday.' He picked up the keys of his bike and ordered with a flick of his finger. "Come with me."

"And what about me, Sir?" DD asked.

He grunted with displeasure upon being reminded he had two of us to be worried about. "Alternate days," he suggested, scratching his beard. "We can't ride triples."

A nonplussed DD returned to an empty cubicle outside his cabin while I asked Jalan on our way to the garage. "Where are we going?"

His answer blew my socks off. "Kalyan."

'Tell my mother I love her,' I whispered to the wind as the bike took off on its journey towards eternity. The engine was a roast, the roads were bumpy, and by the time we reached the first doctor's clinic in Kalyan, I thought I could do with a prescription of Sulfamylon for soothing my posterior.

The doctor was busy, and when he learnt from his receptionist that two medical representatives were here to hard-sell their company's drugs at his clinic, he got busier. For the hour or more that we cooled our heels in the waiting room, Jalan showed no signs of being in a hurry.

"You did tell me we have to visit several doctors every day," I said, looking at my watch. "It is noon already and we are still at our first."

He shrugged. "We do what we can do."

"And what if this doctor refuses to take our pitch?" I asked.

"Then we offer him incentives," Jalan said, smiling for the first time in the thirty-six hours that I had known him.

Once we were summoned inside the doctor's room, though, a different personality took over Jalan. He bounced and pranced, pleaded and joked with the doctor, and spoke to him like he was addressing a long-lost friend. Midway through the conversation, when the doctor indicated he would 'give it a thought' because other drug makers were offering similar compositions at discounted rates, Jalan threw in his final and most effective salvo.

"But the other drug makers will not offer your family a discounted holiday to Europe." He grinned for so long, I had enough time to count the different colours of the palette that belonged to each of his teeth.

We emerged from the clinic victorious. The doctor promised Jalan a deal in which he could happily report back to his bosses and get a pat on the back, if not a raise. But once we were out of that room, he had reverted to his morose self who quietly started his bike with the sole motive of finishing his work for the day and getting back home without much fuss and fanfare.

When I asked him why he did not seem suitably happy, he responded with the only valuable advice he gave me over the course of my entire assignment. "Never get too emotional about your job."

At the end of a weeklong slew of field visits, I had gained some understanding of Salesforce and several darker tones of skin. DD and I reported back to Jalan's cabin early the following week so we could know what we were now required to do.

"Non-field, I assume," we said together, hoping this was the last of field trips we would be subjected to.

He said something vague and dispassionate that sounded like "Draw inferences from the sales reports I have emailed you and suggest measures to increase the bottom line and Where Do You Come From Where Do You Go Where Do You Go, Oh Cotton Eye Joe..." before his voice dropped and he left the office complaining of a severe headache. For another fortnight he stayed MIA. No one in the office knew much about what he was up to.

"He does this often," someone muttered before asking us 'not to quote them.'

With few counsellors or guides who could help us understand the task of the assignment better, we resorted to what we were best at looking up the internet and searching random white papers on Marketing and Sales Trends that we could borrow snippets and graphs from and replace with random numbers from Jalan's sales reports. Even as we dolled up our reports with fancy jargon and sexy graphs, something in my bones told me this was not a college assignment and anyone with half a notch of keener interest in this assignment than Jalan would call bullshit on whatever it was we were doing. However, something was better than nothing and hence we pasted liberally from case studies and white papers sources from the Wonderful Web while dealing with a sick feeling in the gut that our Copy & Paste act wouldn't go down well with Jalan when he returned. Until the snake reared its ugly hood, we stuck ours in the sand, taking liberal lunch breaks in the canteen and post-lunch recuperation breaks at the benches by the big beautiful fountains of the estate.

But a fortnight later, my worst fear came true. It also happened to occur on the day DD had taken ill, which meant I would brave the storm by myself. I sat at my desk, grappling with Google's secondary data sources as I did every day when Jalan walked in with a fresh haircut and a reddened face contoured with multiple frowns that showed signs of severe tension. His jaw dropped low, and beads of sweat formed on his forehead.

Surely there was something more than the summer heat that had been bothering him. "Show me your progress report," he ordered, slapping the cubicle separator fervently.

"The what?"

"Whatever it is you have been working on, you two," he wiggled a finger.

Confused, I handed him a bunch of loose print-outs that documented whatever half-assed observations we had attempted to pass off as Ivy-League-MBA-nuggets.

"Is there an emergency?" My voice trembled. From not giving a rat's butt to hyperventilating over a progress report, Jalan's approach towards us had made a dramatic turn.

"Yes," he squeaked nervously. "Mat called this morning. He is flying up from Singapore and…"

"And?" Mat, or Vimal Mathur, was Jalan's boss, the marketing head for the diabetic division across the Asia Pacific region, and a terror for most people who worked under him. Reportedly, Jalan had borne the brunt of his terror one time too many, and Mat had never felt too happy while doing Jalan's quarterly appraisal.

Unfortunately for Jalan, and indirectly even for DD and me, overseeing our project progress was one of his performance tasks set for him for the coming quarter. "He had asked me for some reports."

"Which became our summer assignment," I said slowly, understanding.

He looked like he was going to nod. Instead, his head spun, his hands scrunched up the print-outs I had handed him with all my love, and he made a paper ball with them and flung it inches short of my face. "What is this nonsense?"

"Nonsense?" I stuttered. I mean I knew it was a lot of nonsense, but I did not expect a dude like Jalan to notice it with one quick look. "You can't call it nonsense, Avinash."

And he certainly couldn't fling a paper ball at me. But he was in no mood to be schooled about civility in the heat of the moment. "Oh, yeah? Would you like to tell Mat that? Because he is going to skin me alive for showing him this tripe!"

Otherwise a meek rat, his words now were loud enough to gather the entire attention of the floor. I seethed with rage at his audacity. For three weeks he had barely bothered to oversee our work, and now that Mat was coming to give him some stick, Rip Van Winkle had decided to wake up and skin me alive.

"What did you think?" He thundered. "That a badge from a fancy B-school will let you get away with anything?"

Now that I smelt envy on him, I wish I could hold and hug him, and whisper softly and reassuringly in his red-hot ear that this fancy B-school was not that fancy and worth boasting about and that he had not missed out on much. But he marched back to his cabin fuming before I could even finish wincing. With the earth now caving beneath me, I felt a cloud of humiliation around me as a hundred eyes looked at me from across the floor with sentiments ranging from sympathy to amusement. I hung my head in shame all day and waited for the evening so I could get the hell out of there. At the stroke of five, I ran out, feeling an intense desire to vomit on the freshly sparkled marble floors of the VRF lobby.

I dumped the cab tonight and walked to Haji Ali. An hour of one of the loneliest and darkest walks I had ever endured until I decided to call Naina. "I need to meet you."

"What's up, boy?" she asked in her usual, cheerful voice. "No hi or hello, getting right on to a demand, eh?"

"Friends forever, remember?" I asked.

"Yes, of course," she sobered a little. "What is the matter? You sound harried."

"I *am* harried."

"Don't be," she ordered. "Where are you? I will first hear you out and then ask you why today is the first time you have bothered to contact me since summer training started. Done?"

"Haji Ali seaside," I replied.

"Haji Ali?" she sounded surprised. "What are you doing there?"

"Feeding pigeons," I said, my voice now ready to break. "Just come. Please."

She sighed. "Be cool, Nakul. I will see you there."

She hopped out of a taxi that pulled over at the kerb twenty minutes later, with a slow grunt. She wore an office blazer matched perfectly with pinstriped trousers and beige pumps. Her hair was perfectly tied back in a ponytail. "Wow, you look every bit the high flyer!"

She examined herself from top to bottom with admiration. "I do, don't I?"

"Yeah, I have never seen you look this good," I said.

She hauled herself over the promenade wall and perched beside me as we faced the sea. Handing me one of two cups of cappuccinos brewed at Café Coffee Day, she spoke. "I don't think you have called me here to insult me. And you look like death. What is wrong with you?"

I told her about Jalan's outburst and about how I fantasised about killing him with a chainsaw. "Am I the asshole for wanting to do that?"

She crinkled her nose in disapproval. "So, a superior shouted at you. That's what got your knickers in a bunch?"

"No, a superior who had not bothered to bother about my project for three weeks decided to scream at me one fine day – in front of a hundred people, mind you! – just because his ass was now on the line," I elaborated. "Is that enough to get my knickers in a bunch?"

"Yes, it is," she agreed. "I just don't think you should kill him with a chainsaw." Taking my hand in hers, she said. "Look, now. What others say to you is not always in your control. It is very well in your control though to decide what feedback you pay heed to and what you discard."

"I discard Jalan's feedback," I said sourly. "In fact, I discard him altogether. I declare hereby he is not my boss, and I am not going back to that office again."

"And what feedback will you pay heed to?" she asked.

I arched back to gauge her intention. "Are you about to judge me, Naina?"

She laughed. "I judge you all the time. What makes you think I have not? Today I am asking you if you are willing to take some feedback. For your own betterment."

Notwithstanding the uncomfortable lump I felt in my throat, I nodded. "Go on."

"I think you need to grow up, Nakul."

I ran my palms along my six-foot-tall frame. "How much more, you reckon?"

Slapping my arm, she spoke firmly. "Exactly. This urge to make light of everything. This is a sign you need to grow up. This is just your first – not even an actual job – just an assignment in an organisation. I am glad you got some homily from your supervisor, dude. Maybe it tells you that you need to get a little serious about work. I know it sounds preachy coming from a classmate. But really, your job's going to be a lot harder than our college assignments which I know you mostly gas your way through."

"Rubbish!" I growled. "My assignments are top-notch."

"Because they are prepared by Sameer and Swapnil," pat came her reply. "I have seen the slides you present from their pack: the Introduction and the Table of Contents. And then you do your grand handover: *I will now pass the mic to my dear colleagues Swapnil and Sameer so they can take you through the rest of the pack.* Cheeky bastard, you are."

"Ok," I conceded. "Yes, I might have done that on occasion. But this was the first time I was trying to do something useful. And I got slam-dunked while trying to do it."

"Then go back tomorrow and do better," she said. "If Jalan does not recognise your merit, this assignment will at least prep you for better things once you are out in the real corporate world."

We stared for a while at the darkening sea. At a distance, the evening prayers had started in the mosque. The sky was turning its magenta to black. From a nearby café wafted the aroma of delicious grilled sandwiches. The council had ended. Our words had dried up. But right there in that quiet moment, as we sat idly, I discovered a world of contentment and security. And it was possibly this quiet, accompanied by the stillness of the ocean, that somehow made me believe this moment was going to last forever. That the two years of this glorious campus life would never end. That I could just telephone Naina at my beck and call and she would come running to me with a ready solution to all my problems.

"Can I say something?" My question broke through the comfortable silence that had enveloped us.

She snapped out of her thoughts with a smirk. "Like you have ever asked!"

I rested my tired head on her shoulder, which she patted with her free hand as I felt emboldened to proceed. "This – I don't want my words to be misconstrued."

"Try me."

"I could get used to this," I said, sitting up straight.

"To what?"

"This," I said, motioning towards the little space between us. "This bond. I feel a connection with you, Naina. I don't want it to get…"

"Misconstrued," she nodded, a worried frown forming a deep ridge in her temples. "Yeah, you said. So, get to the point, will you?"

"You are special," I said slowly, careful to let the words drop with extreme caution. "A special kind of special. Not the special that should be attributed to anything romantic. Do you get what I mean?"

She picked up my coffee cup and sniffed its rim. "Did I accidentally mix something in your coffee?"

"Shut up!" I said. "I mean I don't love you. But I depend on you. Immensely."

She diffused the awkwardness with a roll of her eyes. Whether it was because she understood nothing of what I said or understood enough to know that the subject needed to be changed pronto, I could not be sure. "You don't love me? How dare you!"

Without waiting for an answer, she pulled me into a hug again, and I felt no need to explain any further. I surrendered myself to the feeling that this was the most beautiful friendship there could ever be. But amidst my presumptions, I got so carried away that it did not occur to me to enquire if she felt that way too. And from there germinated my biggest mistake that would also tell me I did indeed need to grow up: that I benchmarked everything she did in the future against this seemingly perfect moment which, like the still ocean and the magenta sky that slowly turned black, looked like it would last forever.

16

"Nakul! Do you know what class this is?" I felt Vandana's hands shake me by the shoulders.

I turned around with an ecstatic hurrah. "It has been ages! And look at the gorgeous tan you've got! The Delhi summer has done you some good, after all!"

"And me?" Aryan poked his face in between and bared his teeth, holding a Happydent in a grin.

"Boy, you were already tanned," I replied. "Now you are charred."

"But not for nothing," he said. "Do you know what a fine summary report my boss wrote about me? How did yours go?"

My heart sank on hearing the question. Thankfully Vandana did not give me a chance to dwell on it too long. "First answer my question. What are you doing in this class? Don't tell me you chose Finance for your Minors!"

"By way of elimination," I offered a sheepish smile. "It was better than choosing Finance for Majors. Marketing combined with Finance, guys! I think it is the best plan that goes with my career path."

"Career path!" Aryan chuckled. "So, you finally found it, eh?"

"Even if I did not get as fancy a summary report as my esteemed friend here," I smiled.

"Oh yes!" He remembered again. "So how did it go?"

"I survived."

I told them about the ordeal we went through in our final presentation. DD and I were split up into different rooms. He had come out of his presentation a happy man; hence I had not felt the need to ask him how he had fared. But I, on the other hand, had been grilled by the Marketing Executives of VRF Pharma as though I was singularly responsible for the one per cent drop in their share prices that year. To my good fortune, one of the panel members was kinder than the others; he had also ascended to the role of Marketing Director – West Zone in no time and I assumed he, did not, unlike the others in the room, feel the urge to enhance his importance by taking a hapless summer trainee to task.

"A good start," he told me later. "But you know you have a lot to work on. Do not worry; we will send your institute a report as favourable as possible."

"All is well that ends well, then," said Vandana. "Now on to Year 2. Let us put the past behind us."

We ushered ourselves into the Consumer Marketing classroom where our second academic year was set to be flagged off. Mrs Nilima Agarwal, christened 'Siren' by the students, greeted us with a loud and shrill *Good Morning* before embarking on a breathless rhapsody about her Marketing adventures in her early career days in the nineties, how she was instrumental in devising *that* popular campaign and launching *those* nifty products when few mavericks were ready to disrupt the market with their innovation and risk-taking appetite. Her moniker was attributed to her ability to pierce our eardrums with her sharp sound waves. For some reason, she had been given to understand there was an altogether different reason she was called 'Siren' and she could never stop gushing about it.

When she finally left at the strike of the third hour, we bounded out of the room like school children running out at the gong of the school bell. Our usual table at the canteen awaited us, our snug group of six that waited to reunite after eight weeks of bittersweet separation that brought us all closer to each other. We began catching up on all the scoops we had missed telling each other. Everyone had their own summer stories to recount; especially Aryan, who had been trying to convince us for a long time that he had been lauded for his innovative idea to sell the company's latest snack item in plastic jars of different SKUs, and that he had been offered a pre-placement offer by his boss. Just then, for the first time since I had set foot on this campus, a face presented itself and took my world by storm. She had to be a college junior, I knew. Or else I would have seen her before. She had sharp features, skin as smooth as ivory, and a cute dimple that ran miles deep into her adorable cheeks.

"Guys," I tapped our table nervously. "Please cast a subtle glance at 45 degrees. Anyone knows who that is?"

"Where? Who?" Sameer shouted, as excited as a toddler who had found a jar of jellies.

"Down, boy!" I cautioned him with a shush. "She just looked here. Shush."

Vandana, paying no heed to a concept called volume control, thought of making it clear to everyone just in case they had not seen her. "He is talking about the girl in the floral print top and white denim and – oh by God, the most gorgeous ruby earrings I have seen!"

'She With The Ruby Earrings' had now most definitely heard us because she looked back right at us while staying hooked to a phone call that she was taking. If there was any room to embarrass me any further, Aryan filled it up by pointing a lazy finger in her direction.

"Oh, her! Yes, I see her."

I dug my face in my hands lest she sees my tomato-red cheeks flush with shame. Kicking Aryan in the shin, I grunted. "Quiet, you stupid monkey! Now, look what you have done!"

She left soon. I hoped it was because her work there was done and she had no interest in exchanging coy looks with me, and not because we had made it amply obvious she was the subject of our discussion.

"Don't call me a monkey," Aryan complained. "If anything, I helped you with the PR. She might now give you some attention to find out why you were giving her all that attention. This is how it always works."

"Says the guy who has never scored with a girl," Naina said, somewhat dourly. "Seven-point-five, tops. Don't see what the big deal was about her anyway."

"Unfair," said Sameer. "Why would you cut two-point-five?"

"Alright she is Miss Universe," Swapnil said finally. "Now will someone tell me what the plan for the day is?"

"The beach?"

Vetoed.

"Dine out?"

Vetoed. Too repetitive and boring.

"The movies?"

Vetoed, too. We had watched them all already.

"We have to do *something*," Swapnil said.

"Why do we have to meet anyway?" Naina asked. Once again, I could not help but notice irritation in her tone. "If it is another of your questionnaires you need to be filled out for some corporate project, count me out, boss."

She saw our wide, angry eyes stare at her and that only annoyed her even more. 'What is the problem?'

"Nothing," I said with a wave of the hand.

Swapnil waited until Sameer led Vandana out under the pretext of asking her to accompany him to the ATM across the gate. "Naina! How can you not remember? It is Vandana's birthday tomorrow. We want to plan a surprise for her. Let us get her a cake."

Naina frowned, struggling to remember – and then winced when she finally did. "I think I need a nap. Yes, let's plan to meet. Just let me know whatever."

"On our hostel terrace," said Swapnil.

"Are you out of your mind?" I countered. "Girls can't set foot inside."

"We will make arrangements," he winked.

"Ok guys," Naina said, picking up herself and her satchel. "Just text me once you have decided."

"What's with her?" Aryan asked after she had left.

"Let me find out," I said, running after her.

She had just hailed a rickshaw and had hopped into it when I managed to catch up with her. "Are you alright? You seemed a little disoriented."

The frown still rested on her forehead. "Yeah, I will be lying if I said I was not. Listen, are you up for catching up before we meet for Vandana's celebration?"

'Wow, let me think. I had a tedious assignment on Product Marketing lined up for submission the next day. No, Naina. I cannot catch up with you. I need some discipline instilled in my life and I am sorry but finding time for friends has no room in my discipline rulebook.'

"Of course," I said. "Just tell me the time and place."

"I will text you," she said, asking the driver to get going.

I found Aryan and Swapnil outside the canteen when I returned. "Is everything ok?"

"She seemed a bit unusual," I said. "But she said we had nothing to worry about. So, that is that."

"Call her," Aryan suggested. "She might tell you things she won't tell us."

I did not want to tell him I already knew that was true. But his acknowledgement of my special privilege of being a close confidant to her filled me with a strange sense of satisfaction, which was disrupted only by Aryan motioning towards the quad again.

"Why, your Lady Love has found her friends!"

I turned around and saw 'The Girl With Ruby Earrings' now standing with five boys from her batch. Away from pesky seniors like me and in the company of her real friends she smiled a lot more, I noted. But it drove me insanely jealous to imagine I was not part of her circle.

"Let us go rag them all," Aryan said, reading my mind. We will shoo the boys away."

"Yes," Swapnil agreed. "It will be hard for Nakul to lose if he is the only contender."

"You can't be sure!" Aryan chuckled before getting kicked in the shin again.

The sea was dead calm that evening. The waves stopped hundred-odd metres ahead of where Naina and I sat. Yet the gentle sound of water crashing against the sand was audible thanks to the pin-drop silence that we had kept for the first half hour.

"Are you still in need of a nap?" I finally asked.

"No. I am fine now."

"Then why are you so quiet?"

"I know, it's strange, we haven't spoken at all. Sing a song."

"What?"

"You heard me. I need to get into a better mood. So sing a nice song."

"Look here, Naina," I said, "I know pretty well we are not here to sing songs. So, over with it and let it out now."

"I've been a little worried since morning," she finally began. "Ramchandran is creating some trouble for me in my summer project grading."

Ramchandran, or Ramu – the abbreviation being more of a convenience than a sign of affection - was a Finance whiz and a professor who classified his students into two pools- the pro-Ramu philosophy and the anti-Ramu philosophy. While most students chose to enter the first pool out of fear of the Ramu phenomenon, there were a few adventurous ones who volunteered to register themselves for the latter by having publicly raised questions against his concepts. Naina happened to be one of those unfortunate scapegoats who bleated a bit too blatantly in one of his classes in the last trimester of the first year. She had got into his bad books already, and to add to her misfortune, he was the internal faculty assigned to guide her in her summer project, which also meant that he would be grading her project.

"What is he up to?" I asked.

"He told me that my findings of the project were frivolous and based on inadequate research, and if he were me, he wouldn't even bother to submit such an ineffective report. Imagine the wretch!"

"Just like that?" I shook my head in disbelief. "Without giving you reasons for his feedback?"

Her moist eyes glistened in the moonlit night. "There is history. When we were at summer training, he had asked me to provide him with a weekly update on how I was tracking at work. I found it odd that he did because no other faculty member I know has hounded their students for interim report updates. I still did email him every week, until one day…" Her voice was now jarred. The words crumbled slowly out of her mouth. "Until one day he crossed the line."

My fingers froze. I curled them into my fists to keep them warm while I searched for the right words to react to a situation I had little understanding of. "Did he…misbehave with you?"

She responded with a smirk that said it all. "Misbehaviour is a subjective term. Especially when applied to a man. He asked me to come to his cabin one evening after I was to finish work at Summers. On an evening when we did not officially have any classes. When he and I both knew there would not be a single soul on campus. What would you call that, Nakul?"

"What a cheapskate!" I snarled. "I am sure you refused."

"And that has manifested in what we are seeing today," she explained. "Ramu will have his revenge."

"Oh no, he will not!" I said, getting up. "We will call him out."

"It is not your battle to fight," she said quietly. "Sit down, Tiger."

"Oh, it is my battle alright," I stook akimbo. "If it is yours, it is mine too."

Something stirred up inside of her. She looked up at me with an irritation I had not seen before. "No, it is *not*. Don't try and be a hero when I am not asking you to be one, ok? The role of a friend is to be a sounding board, which I thought you would be. If I needed you to be a crusader for my cause, I would tell you. Now if I am asking for you to draw a boundary, you will honour it. Get it?"

Seeing the colour drain off my face, she snapped. "What?"

"I was just trying to help," I mumbled, taken aback.

"And you are," she calmed down again. "By being here next to me. That is the help I need."

She was underplaying what impact the sleazebag had had on her. She knew that I knew it even if I nodded in response. Because she proceeded to clarify. "I am not the only one. Or so I have heard. I spoke to Ms Dubey in the Accounts Department and she told me – rather coolly, to my surprise – that I could not get any action taken against him if I wanted. He is a veteran of this college and is highly veneered."

"So, now?"

"So, now I let him bulldoze my effort on the Summer Project," she smiled and winced at the same time. "Let him. What harm will one bad grade cause me against plenty of good ones? Ramu is not going to decide my future."

But I had a good mind to decide Ramu's future, I wanted to tell her. Now that she had drawn a line in the sand as far as my role in the matter was concerned, I did not want to spell it out before her. But a restlessness now rose in me and I felt ill at ease to continue sitting there whiling away time.

Then, reading my mind like she'd read the nutritional information label on a bottle of jam, she thickened her words. "You will do nothing."

"Of course,' I said, looking away. 'Your battle to fight, and all that."

"We have a deal, yeah?"

I fetched a pen from the pocket of my jeans. Uncorking the cover, I asked in earnest. "Where do I sign?"

"Idiot," she flicked sand at my face. "Now, let us run and give Vandana some big birthday bumps."

"I have some urgent work to finish in my room," I said. "You head to the terrace when it is time. The guys will meet you at the gate and lead you upstairs."

Back in my room, I moaned once again on seeing Swapnil's unwashed clothes that had now accumulated to form a chair of their own. Time being of the essence, I sat on the mound of unappealing fabric and fired my laptop on. Embarrassed at my lack of ingenuity, I formed an email id: upsetstudent83@gmail.com and started composing the one and only email the account would ever hold.

Dear Dean Sir,

I am writing from an anonymous email ID because I'd rather not tell you my real name. It makes me uncomfortable, and I can tell you it is not even important.

This email is to bring to your attention a matter of grave concern for your kind action...

18

"**N**o!" The guard manning the hostel gate exclaimed. "You know this is not in my hands." For a moment he frowned uncomfortably at Naina before dropping his stare downward, muttering something to himself about the audacity with which inmates approached him with vulgar requests.

"Ratan Bhai," we cajoled him, "it is a birthday celebration. You can't deny us that, can you?"

He dropped his shoulders in despondence. "I had my birthday last week. I stood here all night doing what I have been asked to do. Why would I change the rule for you?"

Swapnil looked at his watch, leaning towards Sameer. "I trust your persuasion skills with this. Aryan and I need to go pick up the cake and the birthday girl."

"I will stay with him," I said, turning again to face Ratan Bhai with puppy eyes who now stood in defiance with his arms crossed over his chest.

"No," he grunted softly in pre-emption of another plea.

Sameer, not one to lose time in excessive beseeching, did next what a rich inheritor of a family business was best at producing a crisp currency note. He placed it in Ratan's shirt pocket and patted it comfortingly even as I baulked in fright and disapproval.

"That is just an assault on his self-respect," I whispered, to which he nodded regretfully.

"Yes, I know," he whispered back to me, "but we have no option and no time."

Ratan mumbled a while longer about how spendthrift youngsters like us had the option to celebrate midnight birthday soirees at JW Marriott rather than risk his reputation at his job. We told him we were not *as rich* as he thought we were (true for me, Sameer went on to contest my rebuttal because how dare I tell anyone Sameer was not rich) and that we fancied the midnight terrace with its band of mosquitoes and the soft moonlight a lot more than the mahogany-scented lobby of JW Marriott. Then, absently contouring the seams of his pocket that guarded the bribe, he let us in.

"If someone finds out…" his voice fell.

"Nobody will," Sameer assured him. "Just let us in through the rear."

He led us to the rear of the hostel and to a small awning that opened into the guard room. It was a tiny enclosure with modicum furnishings. A damp stench from poor ventilation filled the air in the room. A small wooden cot lay in one corner, and beside it lay a table fan with a broken blade on a tripod with a broken leg. There was but one small grilled window that would cast a small splash of sunlight during the day only sufficient to keep the room one degree below pitch darkness. And I thought once again of the money that we conveniently stuffed into his pocket without any qualms.

"This just makes me feel miserable," I said to Sameer as we were ushered in. "Do you see that? The poor guy does not even have a decent fan to cool him on a stuffy night."

Sameer lobbed his neck to a side, an expression he used often to convey his frustration. "You are right. Let us just go back. And take that money right out of his pocket, yeah?"

"Smart ass," I shoved a fist into his back to prod him.

We found our way up to the terrace through a thin spiral wooden staircase beginning from Ratan's room. The wood had peeled off the corners of the stairs and they yielded a loud creak with each step we placed on them. The staircase moaned under the pressure of my abundant mass and I feared a bad fall lest it would give way. We ambled up as fast as possible to the top, till we reached a cobweb-decorated iron door that opened into the rear side of the terrace. The patio boasted elaborate arrangements that would suit a grand celebration. A laptop was placed on a table at the side, fitted with a pair of speakers. The decision to bring in music with speakers was taken after due deliberation, given the possibility of attracting unwanted attention from the other students in the hostel. But then again, the plan was well-calculated. Being just the beginning of the new academic year after summer, several students had taken an extended vacation after training and had not returned from home. Moreover, that happened to be a Friday night, which meant a good number of guys had either hit the movie hall for the latest film in town or were out clubbing or pubbing. Aryan and I had sat laboriously through the afternoon, burning a compilation of the choicest songs from our music library. Pizza packets from Domino's were stacked on a separate table, and beside the stack lay a crate of premium vodka and whisky, handpicked by Sameer.

After a long ride in an autorickshaw and the slow, painful climb of the staircase, there was no reason for Vandana to not have figured out a surprise birthday party was in order. But being the sweetheart that she was, she put on a reasonable affectation of surprise and awe by rolling her eyes into big ovals and covering her mouth with her hands when she saw the others waiting for her on the terrace. Birthday hugs were exchanged with assurances of how she had been taken by surprise and that she had been wondering why the boys were walking her up a decrepit staircase of their hostel.

Aryan thrust a breadknife into her hand and nudged her towards the cake. "Everyone is very hungry. Feed us first. Act surprised later."

After we tore through the cake like savage beasts, I was about to assault the boxes of pizza when Sameer stopped me, rolling the crate of drinks forward. "Not so fast. Let us all raise a toast to Vandana."

"No ale?" I peered into the crate with disappointment. "You know I can't get past a pale ale."

"All boundaries will be violated tonight," he said to me. "Look at the birthday girl!"

Vandana, with a bottle of vodka vertically dispensed over her mouth, winked at me. "Do it for friendship. Come on!"

I turned to Swapnil, the last teetotaller standing in the group. He shrugged. "Your call."

"For friendship?" I asked him.

Without waiting for him to respond, I took a swig of vodka for the first time in my life. Despite it ravaging my food-deprived gut like a fire does a haystack, the drink grew on me as I was egged on. "Can you mellow it a little?" I slurred minutes later.

"Gladly!" Sameer poured me a glass of one part vodka and four parts Sprite. The intensity decreased but the quantity kept increasing through the night. Before I knew it, I was a sloppy, emotional mess spreading myself one part on the floor and four parts on the shoulders of my friends.

"I can't believe this will all be over soon," I wept.

"Sameer, you are so sick!" Naina laughed. "You got him drunk so you could have a good laugh at the emotional fool, eh?"

Drunk as I was, I latched on to the label instantly. It may have been the liquor pushing the sentiment in overdrive, but 'emotional fool' sounded hurtful and disrespectful. I let it slide as a once-off remark even as Vandana pushed a slice of pizza down my throat to calm my senses down.

"Nothing is getting over soon," she reassured me, wrapping an arm around me. "We are leaving campus in a year. Not each other."

"Amen!" Aryan raised a glass in a toast.

"Are you guys for real?" Naina smirked again, then laughed for cover. "Ok, sorry. Yeah, Amen!"

"Why did you say that?" Sameer asked.

"Nothing."

"No, come on, tell us," I encouraged her. "It is ok, Naina. We can stomach a disagreement."

"I wish there is no disagreement on this," she said. "I wish what she just said is true. That we are not leaving each other. It just…sounds Utopian. You have seen that cute junior on campus this morning, Nakul Kapoor! Who knows you might be leaving all of us for her tomorrow itself!"

"Nonsense!" I roared. I was about to issue a lengthy argument, but through my blurry eyes, I strained to gauge a sign of envy in her. I saw none.

Just to be doubly sure, I staggered over to her and leaned against the parapet of the wall she had her back to. Softening my question against the chatter the others had resumed, I quietly spoke. "Are you ok with that?"

"With what?" she asked.

"With me taking an interest in what's-her-name?" I asked.

I wondered if I had already been knocked out of my senses and if my question was incoherent because instead of envy or irritation, I saw a befuddled look on her face. "Why would I not…" she began, and then the penny dropped. "Nakul Kapoor – do you think I am in love with you?"

"I'll be damned if I thought you were," I stuttered, realising now I was making a complete fool of myself. "But it never hurts to find out and be certain."

"What if I help you on your quest to get in touch with your Dimple Doll?" she suggested. "Will that convince you I have no issues with you hitting it off with her?"

"A simple *No* in response will do just fine," I assured her, at which she burst out laughing to the point, she nearly choked on her drink. Even as I patted her back to help her catch her breath, I asked myself what could be so possibly absurd about my question. Sure, we both knew we were great friends. There had never been a hint of a romantic liaison. I knew there never would be one. I had never considered a romantic connection with her, and I was nearly certain she would happily friendzone me too. But the depth of my bond with her – or at least what I felt of it – caused me to at least imagine that this friendship was easy to get misinterpreted for something higher.

"Sorry," she said while stifling her laughter. "Look at you! Ok, let me cut this short Nakul. Of course, I have no issues with you dating – oh wait let me not get ahead of myself – with you speaking to that girl. That is not what I meant."

"Then what did you mean?" I asked. "When you said it all sounded fantastical?" "Merely that as much as I love you," she started, and then raised her voice, gathering everyone's attention, "as much as I love you all, I don't think this is the be-all and end-all of my life. Or your lives for that matter. We will meet more friends, associates, and colleagues. The wheels of life will keep moving. Why would I agree we will all still be as we are tonight?"

Sameer cupped his hands, simulating a trumpet. "The wise one has spoken! The matter is now sub-judice."

"Let us drink to that!" Naina raised a glass even as my intent stare at her queer arguments was not lost on her. "What, do you think I have had one too many?" she asked with a giggle.

"I think you have," I said, unsure if it was the intoxication driving the hurt or the other way around.

"I may have," she said with a wink. "But I can promise you I will stand by every word even when I see you in the morning."

"Be that as it may," I slurred, my voice dropping in tandem with my sight. Just before the lights before my eyes shut out for the night, I caught a glimpse of Swapnil, sitting cross-legged in the circle, his hands-free of any drink or food. A quiet, contemplative smile hung on his lips as he looked at me with sympathy.

"Why don't I see you drinking?" I asked.

"Because I don't drink," came the reply. "You know I don't."

"Saala, ditcher!" I swung at the air between us. "A toast was raised to our friendship, was it not?"

He laughed, moving his hands in a clean circular motion. "Did you not hear Naina? The wheels of life and something like that?"

And then I slept like a baby. It did not matter that the floor was damp or that the music was loud or that the mosquitoes were pesky. My BAC had spiked to unprecedented levels, rendering me weightless, letting me float on a dreamy cloud of – what was the word again? *Utopia.* I don't remember how long I slept. But right ahead of the crack of dawn, I was awoken by The Voice.

I sat up with a start, feeling my parched mouth and my saliva-stained jaw with disdain. The others were still next to me, but not one of them was awake. "Who is it?"

"Can we talk?" asked The Voice.

I stared at my friends who were sprawled on the floor like sheepskin. "Ok, this is creepy."

"Just listen to me," it said again. "Having a good time?"

"Yes, I was so far," I said, my eyes now scanning the sky.

"What do you think of the wheels of life spiel you got from your friend?"

I sighed sharply. So, it had all really happened. "I make nothing of it. Naina had no idea what she was talking about. Look at all these miserable drunks!"

Really?" It tested me. "Or maybe she made perfect sense, and you just did not want to ingest it. Maybe because you have your head right up your..."

"Someone rightly said that logic is the ruin of the spirit," I said. "I am therefore listening to my heart."

"I am sure no one ever said that," said The Voice. "You just made that shit up. The spirit that does not follow logic, in fact, is condemned for eternity into a deep black hole."

Ok, that was it. Despite myself, I crawled on all fours towards the music system. Turning the volume up a few notches, I looked up at The Voice again. "Thank you for the uncalled-for sermon. Now if you don't mind, I love this song."

"*Comfortably Numb,*" It noted. "Hmm. Do you know what it means?"

"What what means?"

"Comfortably numb."

I shrugged. "You will tell me, I am sure."

"It is what you will feel the day you learn to contend with your friend's opinion," it said. "That the wheels of life will keep moving. That at the end when you look around, you are all alone."

The Voice was gone. Staggering, the others gradually stood on their feet. They talked about what a splendid night, a splendid party it had been. The best night of everyone's lives. Six friends living it up in each other's company, caring two hoots about the wheels of life. For a moment I wandered back to the cryptic warning I had heard: *that at the end when you look around, you are all alone.* But alone, I was not. I nodded at them – yes, the best night of my life too. My heart was a flamingo that flapped away, high up into this beautiful Utopian sky.

19

"Who is Nakul Kapoor?"

Until our college peon rocked up at the door of our classroom with this question, it was an ordinary day of ordinary people with extraordinary dreams ramming their heads against a business case contest announced by an institute in Delhi. Now, this question had brought with it an extreme bout of anxiety to me and a sense of awe to others who marvelled at my name being beckoned from the Dean's office.

But I needed a little context to the request. With a frail heart, I replied, "Me. What is this about?"

The peon did not speak a word. Curling his left fingers in a summon and crawling his right fingers through his shirt buttons to give his chest a nice scratch, he blinked to let me know he was unwilling to share further information at this stage and that I should quietly walk. Like a convict.

The air in Dean Anil Mehra's room was cold and deathly. The silence that engulfed me as I sat on the edge of a chair was punctured by the sound of a flush from inside his toilet. He emerged with a handkerchief meticulously wiping water off his hands as he said 'Stay seated' which was almost funny because I was anyway seated and was too nervous to stand up in greeting.

"Nakul Kapoor," he said. "How is your course coming along?"

"Very well, Sir." If he had started with small talk, maybe there was something benign about this meeting after all.

"What subjects have you elected for?" he asked.

I did not know where this was going, but it still sounded benign enough. "Marketing and Financial Management, Sir."

"IT?"

"No IT, Sir," I said.

He sat in his chair, examined me with pity and clucked his tongue. "What a shame! I wish you had taken IT, Kapoor. Who knows you might have learnt some basics about how easy it is to track an IP address."

My shoulders dropped in resignation. I drew a sharp breath as I stopped myself from telling him that yes Sir, I know an IP address can be traced to assigned laptops but I had just gone out on a punt assuming you'd be too busy to track down an anonymous email address and might instead focus on the problem at hand.

But Anil Mehra was squarely unhappy with my approach. "I am not a fan of rats. You got a problem, you book an appointment with me and come talk to me directly."

Now that the gloves were off, I saw value only in coming clean and coming to the point. "I am sorry, Sir. It was a bad tactic but my intent is clear."

"So, you have a grouse against Ramachandran."

"A grouse might be an understatement, Sir," I said. "In all honesty, I would call that sexual harassment."

"The board will be a judge of that!" His voice rose in a gesture of authority seeking to tell me I needed to stay in my lane. "Not me, and definitely not you, kid. But let me assure you I take such complaints very seriously. I still have a question for you – whose voice, or voices, are you representing?"

My voice thickened in a firm stance. "I cannot tell you that."

"Then I cannot help you."

"The complainant requests anonymity."

"Anonymity!" He raised his hands in the air, then relented. "Ok, I get that. But your complaint is unsubstantiated and not something I can take to the board. Until we get rid of the anonymity clause, of course. What I can do is call Ramachandran and give him wind about something that could be brewing against him. He is a fully grown adult and I expect he takes the hint and mends his ways."

"Thank you, Sir," I said. "I hope it helps."

"Is there anything else I can help you with?" he asked.

I shook my head and stood up to leave when he called out to me. "The complainant must be glad to have you as a friend."

I don't know if the complainant was glad but she was surely very intuitive. For, when I swung the Dean's door open to fan the sweat running down my aching temples, she stood outside with anger that needed no words of introduction.

"What had he called you for?" She started, then closed her eyes and raised a hand. "Don't even try to answer it."

"General stuff," I replied hurriedly while trying to sneak away. "It is not what you think."

"Yeah, general stuff!" She mocked. "Because Mehra is your Uncle, isn't he?"

I swerved around to look her in the eye. "Let me put this frankly, Naina. You have been a little cranky lately, which is okay. But you can't talk down to me like that on one day, and then call me to share your problems on another. Some mutual respect, maybe, yeah?"

"I am sorry for troubling you with my problems," she said.

"No, don't go there!" I stopped her. "You know that is not trouble for me. I am just asking you to cool down. I am standing up to the tone you are taking with me now and I want you to know I will have none of it. So talk to me when you are calm."

I stormed out of the corridor as I heard her yell back at me. "I told you it is my battle to fight!"

I ran out to the quadrangle where Aryan sat at a table with his floater-clad feet perched on the chair opposite his. With a pen dangling from his mouth like a cigar, he contemplatively flipped pages of a handout. "Welcome. I have been waiting. Why is your face so white? Don't tell me it has something to do with the visit to the Dean."

"Yes and no," I said, distracted. "Let us not talk about it. Remind me why am I here?"

He dropped his jaw, shook his head and flipped the handout on the table so I could see the heading. "You have really seen a ghost, haven't you?"

I picked up the handout and threw my head back, remembering. "The business plan contest, yes! I may have forgotten for a moment, brother. But you will be very impressed to know I made some preparatory notes overnight that will blow your mind."

He tilted his head towards me and smiled. "Go on. Blow it."

Swatting his head away, I said. "Now that you know me for a while, do you think I can start working with you on anything until I have found us some…"

"Food," he completed for me, getting up. "Yes, let us get you some food."

We walked out to the dosa-and-sandwich stall outside our college, where blue and white canopies stood to shield customers from the scorching heat of summer but not from the fat flies breeding over the sewage line that ran behind it. We ordered our favourite grilled sandwiches with cheese and jam served on either side. As we gently slapped the little pests away with our hands, from the little awning between my eyes and a waving palm, I saw the dimpled girl from the junior batch again. With two mini hoola-hoops for a pair of purple earrings, she wore a matching purple top over white linen trousers and a pair of flats. The radiance of her skin was second only to the blaze of the afternoon sun. Her eyes, lined with kohl, were damp at the rims as she fought the spices that had been thrown onto her chilly dosa. Undeterred, she chewed on until the tears escaped the wells of her eyes and streamed down her face with remnants of the kohl in little black streams.

"Will you always just stare?" I heard Aryan's faint whisper fall on my cold shoulder.

Shaking my head, I grabbed a bottle of mineral water from the counter and stepped towards her. The guy behind the counter snubbed me with a reminder that it was not for free, in response to which Aryan slammed a tenner onto his palm and said, "Timing, boss!" And the man behind the counter understood immediately. *Matters of the heart*, he nodded.

"Too spicy?" I debuted in the game of Making A Move as I uncorked the bottle and offered it to her.

Surprised yet grateful, she took a sip of the water; realising it was not enough, she then downed half the bottle before returning it. "Saved me. Thanks!"

I retreated half a step but lingered. Enough to keep the conversation going but not enough to make my desperation apparent. Over my shoulder, I sensed Aryan holding out our paper plates with sandwiches that were now ready. "I am Nakul, by the way. And that's my friend Aryan."

"Ruchi." She extended her palm in a handshake, the softness of her hands sending me a crude reminder of how calloused my hands had got after years of unsuccessful endeavours at weightlifting.

Noticing her nose was still ruddy red, I offered her a bite of my sandwich. "The sugar should calm you down."

Tugging lightly at my collar, Aryan spoke through gritted teeth. "Ok stop, doggie. Your tongue is drooling now."

I could not agree more. I felt abashed. Thankfully, she broke a bite off the corner and popped it in her mouth. Maybe out of politeness if not out of need. "Thank you. Any tips to survive the first year?"

Acutely unconscious of my lack of authority to comment on academic discipline, I rattled off as though speaking through a taped recording. "The load can get to you at times. But it is just a matter of meticulousness that can go a long way in balancing your life outside and inside the classroom."

The advice threw Aryan's oesophagus out of whack as a large blob of sandwich got lodged in his throat, sending him into a violent bout of cough. I thwacked his back in rapid succession; first to get the food down to his stomach and then to warn him to get over it.

Recovering, he sputtered slowly. "Yes, Nakul has exemplified time management for his friends."

I made up for the quarter piece of sandwich I had sacrificed to Ruchi by flicking a half of Aryan's. "Excessive carbs make you say silly things, stud. Calm down."

Determined to road-roll my first chance at striking a meaningful conversation with the lady, he said. "We really should be getting back to that business plan. Just saying it for the sake of your, ahem, meticulousness."

"What the hell was that for?" I shook my hand off his grip violently once we were out of her sight.

"You were about to fall in her lap," he said. "You need to play hard to get."

"Says the guy who has always found it hard to get a girl," I scoffed.

Kneading his fingers into the hollow of my shoulders, he said in his usual spirited manner. "It is because I care for you, doofus!"

"For Doofus…" I started, and he completed it for me. "Is an honourable man!"

And feeling proud of another dumb joke we had cracked between the two of us, we laughed again with reckless abandon. Used to the comfort of each other's company, grateful for the little nothings that made us laugh when we saw the nothings together in perspective. Aryan made it possible for me to feel happy being mediocre. At the cusp of leaving academic life to seek out a living, a friend who let me revel in my mediocrity was a prized treasure.

20

A heavy downpour prompting the cancellation of an afternoon lecture on Financial Institutions & Markets was a welcome change in the middle of the week.

"Happy Hump Day!" I said in relief. "Nothing like getting an afternoon off on a Wednesday. I had not even finished my assignment."

We were gliding down the stairs from our classroom down to the lobby. Cleaning her reading glasses with a fibre cloth, Naina quipped. "You don't do your assignments yourself anyway, you child. You get me to do them."

"Yes, exactly what I mean," I said. "You were supposed to help me finish it on Saturday, knock knock! Where had you disappeared after standing me up in the library all evening?"

She looked up at the skies, trying to remember. "Saturday?"

"The child thinks you are growing old," I teased her. "Memory problems? Get some almonds in your diet."

"No, idiot. I remember where I was on Saturday evening," she said. "I was out watching a movie with the Finnies. But I don't remember telling you we would meet in the library."

The Finnies was a term we had assigned to Naina's newfound friends in her Finance major group. I never got around to knowing their names.

But Finnies as a group for easy reference clicked and she happily used the name in regular parlance with me.

"What movie?"

"Bunty Aur Babli."

I bided time to mask my dismay. But my words made no effort to comply. "Did you not also remember you and I had a deal to go watch it together?"

Once again, she looked to the skies for a clue. "Oh shit! Yes, we did. I am so sorry. But you must watch it, yaar. Nice movie."

I bit my lips to stop myself from saying anything. Shaking my head, I was walking away when she pulled me back by the elbow. "Wait. What are you pissed about anyway? That I did not help you with your assignment or that I watched Bunty Aur Babli without asking you to come along?"

"It doesn't matter Naina," I said sourly. "If you don't know, you don't need to know."

"You are being a child!"

The words stung. Not because they were hurtful, but because they were true. I could have kicked myself for being a child, for throwing a fit about something I had no right to fuss about. Yes, she had her own circle of friends too. Yes, to each their own. Yes, it was not a big deal that she stood me up or that she reneged on a movie plan. I could not demand an explanation where none was owed. But there was no easy way to quell this singeing of emotions by a lack of reciprocation for all the times I had been around for her. If only emotional maturity came thick and fast to everyone, the world would see fewer disappointments and heartbreaks. To me, a spoilt brat whose every wish had always been his family's command, a lesson in emotional maturity was a long time coming. And Naina was just beginning to serve me the introductory course.

She caught up with me as I walked out into the rain. "Ok, snap out of it. Let's not be sore. Next movie together."

"I am not sore," I lied. "I need caffeine. Do you?"

"Oh, I need caffeine and then some more!" She rubbed her head. "I have a throbbing headache."

But there was almost nowhere to go. The rain was in no mood to cease. Six hours and counting, this cloudburst was preparing to take the city down. The power supply was cut off. The college, the cafeteria included, had turned into a dark, damp enclosure with daylight very quickly slipping out of its confines. Streams of water that had been getting onto the premises were now growing into ominous pools of slush, grime, and everything the streets nearby brought with them. We were joined now by some more friends who echoed our sentiment that a coffee fix was a matter of utmost urgency. Simply because none of us understood yet the magnitude of calamity unfolding outside the gates.

"I have eaten nothing since morning," Vandana complained.

"So, coffee with food then," Swapnil suggested.

"Very ambitious," I said. "I don't see how we can get a rickshaw to ply through those rivers forming outside."

"Let us just get some biscuits from the provisions store across the road," said Sameer.

"Yeah, that can't be hard," I said, volunteering to go.

Famous last words. Sameer and I rolled up our khakis and waded out onto the road. And then, he said something the triviality of which would be funny a few hours later if it were not for the unfunny situation it would put us in.

"My pants are going to get ruined."

Down the sloped flooring of the campus, we were now caught in a dynamic flow of water, courtesy of an open gutter somewhere in the vicinity. The surface of the flood now tickled our waists. The idiocy of attempting to get to the provision store was well acknowledged by us, but our rumbling stomachs protested. Through the blinding torrent, the provisions store across the road appeared like a hazy mirage, or a giant floatable bobbing up and down in the middle of a sea.

"Now that we are here…" We exchanged a look in the hope that one of us would talk sense into the other and order a retreat.

First, we waded. Then we stumbled. Finally, we swam. An eternity later when we reached the store, the owner was just about to pull down his shutters when he looked at us in disbelief.

"What do you want?"

"Biscuits," we pleaded. "And coffee."

"My stove is soaked," he showed us. "I don't have the heart to tell you how crazy I think you boys are. Here, take some biscuits."

He grabbed whatever packets he could lay his hands on and thrust them onto our palms. We tucked them all inside our shirts – not that it helped much – but soggy biscuits were probably better than no biscuits.

"On a positive note," I gasped for breath as we made our way back through the current, "you don't need to worry about your pants anymore."

When we returned to the college quadrangle, a crowd twice the size of what we had last seen had congregated on the tiny acreage. Passers-by who sought refuge, workers at the food stalls out on the road, and students from the neighbouring colleges who had dared to venture back to their hostels before realising they were not being wise.

"What took you so long?" asked Naina, when we finally found them huddled in a corner.

Sameer looked at me with a smirk. "What shall we tell her, Nakul?"

"That bad?" she asked.

"And more," he replied. "Where is Aryan? Anyone saw him?"

The penny dropped. I cried out in dismay. "Oh, Lord! He was headed to the international airport to lunch with a friend who was on a transit flight."

"Call him!" said everyone, taking turns to dial him before realising all phone networks were jammed.

"Great!" we exclaimed in frustration. "Now we have – God knows how many – stranded friends and hundreds of parents suffering in anxiety when they can't locate us."

"And the media must have blown this out of proportion by now," I said.

"Dude!" Swapnil motioned towards the skies overhead. "There is nothing to blow out of proportion. It is as bad as it can get!"

Meanwhile, it was learnt that a school bus carrying approximately sixty students had fallen into a ditch right outside our institute. The kids were hysterical, and the driver and conductor had cried themselves hoarse for hours trying to get help. Someone from our batch noticed the commotion – thank God for small mercies – and in no time we had formed a rescue group, each of us hauling one child out to safety. We ushered everyone into our dingy but safe haven. Possibly the only day in this institution's history when people were permitted in without the display of an identity card or a visitor's pass. The kids were given a classroom upstairs: the benches were all shoved into a corner. The floor was cold and wet but it made for a bed nonetheless. Food and water continued to remain a problem for several more hours until kind neighbours in the rear alleys of Juhu Scheme came to our aid with several small but warm containers of whatever food they could spin up in a short time. By midnight word had spread around to a good number of families about their children's whereabouts. They were picked up and walked back home. As for the others, they stayed cold but safe.

We slept on hungry bellies and full hearts.

I lie in the pool with my eyes shut. Oblivious to the weather that forebodes an ugly day ahead. Suddenly, a gush of wind topples me off my floating tube, and I fall face-first into the icy water. Like all heavy objects, my portly body starts going down under. I gasp as I try to keep my head above the surface so I can call my friends for help. Naina and Vandana are by the poolside but appear too busy to respond. Naina shakes Vandana hard on the shoulder and asks her to hurry up. "We're getting late," she shows Vandana the watch. I scream again, this time at the top of my voice. She finally turns to me rather indifferently. "Yeah?"

"Help!" I plead.

"We're going downtown and are running late," she says, "my friends are already waiting there. Don't worry, just hang in there. Aryan should be on his way soon."

"I think that's utterly selfish of you," I say.

"Stop being a child! That rope is right on your side. You can hold on to it and come out on your own too. So don't make a big deal out of this."

She's right. There is a rope tied to a lamppost right outside the pool, and the free end of the rope is within my reach. But now anger has overpowered my fear. They disappear, leaving me in the lurch. The pool gradually turns into quicksand, and I am being sucked in real fast. I can either wait for help as I get consumed by the mire, or I need to find a way out on my own. I need to act fast. Real fast...

"Guys, my phone has come alive!" I was awoken the next morning with a start as Vandana celebrated the return of the electric current that travelled through the adjacent socket into her phone charger.

"One lesser problem, that's good." Naina groaned as she stretched out on the floor before sitting up.

Beads of sweat ran down my collarbone. I felt snuffed. Like I had been at the wrong address for a long time and the people inhabiting it were impostors.

"What is the matter with you?" Vandana knelt beside me. "A bad dream?"

I nodded, looking out of the window. The storm had passed. Outside, the ravaged city had come to a standstill. Felled trees, abandoned cars, a dead street dog, and a labourer rowing a shaft, all floated or bobbed along a muddy brown river. The children inside were happier than they had been the previous night. They were being reunited with their families. Our families back home knew now we were alive to recount this tale. But less than two hundred metres off our building, we learnt, a couple had perished in their little hatchback they had been unable to scram out of when the rainwater jammed their doors. The frivolity of my disquiet was disappointing to me as well, and I was in no place to explain it to others.

"It...was not significant."

Vandana tapped me on the knee to regain my attention. "Hey. I have reached out to Aryan too. He is fine. He sought shelter in a Bandra bakery. Says he made do with some leftover pastries and patties!"

"How you wish you had been in his place, eh, Nakul?" Naina tried to make light of my unease even as I exhaled into my palms with relief.

Tight-lipped, I curled my arms over my knees. She exchanged a look; the latter understood and slipped away under the pretext of getting some water.

"You are totally not yourself,' she said. 'Trust me, you can talk about it. Even if it still has something to do about our chat yesterday."

Some friends can see right through you. I offered a half-smile. "I am putting it behind me."

"But not convincingly, I can see," she said. "Can I just ask that we uncomplicate things? I understand where you are coming from. You do the hard yard when I need your support. I have not for once forgotten that. The trouble is you and I are not cut from the same cloth. I might be more callous when I need to be around. It does not mean I don't care. It just means you and I react differently in similar situations."

"And that is ok," I lied. It was not ok. It was practical, realistic, and logical. But it was not ok. "Our friendship is precious." Her voice was earnest. "Let us not wreck it with expectations."

Freewheeling conversations are sometimes harder to digest than sugar-coated platitudes. I could not shake the disillusionment off me. But my response had to allow for a chance to let this precious friendship thrive. "I completely understand. Case dismissed."

21

Two ice cubes stopped clinking in Sameer's third peg of the finest scotch offered in the Happy Times pub. He placed his glass on the table and released a whimper. "I don't want to leave Mumbai! There is no place like this, and there are no friends like you!"

"No repeats for him!" Aryan wagged a finger at us. "I am not carrying him back to the hostel again. Done it once."

"And how is he sure he is leaving Mumbai," I asked the others. "He might get a job here."

Overhearing my question, Sameer lunged in. "No! I am not getting a job here. I am landing a Sales job with Coca-Cola on Day Zero. Delhi for my training, and then I will be at the headquarters in Atlanta before you know it. No job here for me."

Seeing us snigger, Swapnil threw in a note of caution. "This is not his inebriation. He means it. He has been working for it. And for my money, I'd say he is going to make it to Atlanta if he is saying it."

Aryan nudged me in the shin with his foot. "Do you have this kind of vision, brother?"

"Of course," I said. "I will also go to Atlanta one day. On my parents' money."

"No, seriously," Aryan said. "The only memories I have of this place so far are of sleepless nights and bad GPAs. Now with placements around the corner, I have a strong impulse to flee."

"These are the only memories you have, seriously?" I asked.

"That says nothing against what amazing friends you guys have been," he said. "But your friendship ain't coming to my rescue when my father kicks my butt with his favourite one-liner after every examination result is out: *with such grades, I wouldn't accept you as a clerk in my own office.*"

"How classist!" Sameer exclaimed.

"I know!" I chimed in. "Let us leak a word to the clerking community. Unleash them on your father!"

"Classism is one of his virtues," he said almost to himself, "if you compared it against other things he says."

I got my phone out. "Let us call Uncle. Let's tell him – Sir, we are going to have a frank chat."

"He will fly down on a business class ticket to have a frank chat with you,' Aryan said, pushing my phone away. 'Only to knock your self-esteem down like a wall of Jenga."

"You are weeks away from shutting down his concerns forever," Swapnil said reassuringly. "Once you have a job in hand, the GPA argument will go down the annals of history as Irrelevant and Trite."

"And hence my anxiety," Aryan spoke in a cold, sharp sigh. "I just hope I can make it."

I reached for Aryan's hand – not to reassure him but to beg him to not infect me with his anxiety. "Dude. You have been the paragon of calmness in this shitstorm. Don't ruin it now. I need your coolth more than ever. You are going to make it. Get it?"

"Everyone's going to make it," said Swapnil. "Everyone's getting out of here with a job."

"And be grateful your grades are the only thing your folks have a go at you for," Sameer spoke, as though waking from slumber. "Here, I am being pestered with pictures and profiles of prospective brides."

"Isn't that too early?" I asked, careful not to breach any more personal boundaries.

"Too late, as per my family's tradition," he moaned. "I keep getting reminded about it. So when you guys will be out celebrating your final years of bachelorhood with your plush salaries to splurge from, I might just be spending my savings on instant formula and nappies."

"Can I give it a positive spin?" I suggested. "When the rest of us will be struggling to find ourselves a partner, you will have had an instant hook-up facilitated by your family."

"Thanks, but no thanks," he said. "I am done with hook-ups. Soha has..." His voice drowned in another large gulp of Happy Times' fine scotch.

"Disillusioned me." He finished his sentence reluctantly, then threw his head back on his seat and closed his eyes.

Snapping his fingers, Swapnil remarked. "Quick to trust, even quicker to distrust. Why do you have to paint everyone with a broad brushstroke? Not every girl is Soha."

"Yes, there is only one Soha," Aryan said dreamily. Smarting under the sharp glance offered by everyone, he rose to his defence. "What? I can say it now, can't I? Sameer couldn't care less."

"Nazneen is Muslim," Swapnil said after a gap. The name, the first time that we had heard of it, got us all to spring to attention. We stared at him with acute focus. "Yes, I have been seeing someone. Why have I not mentioned it all this time? Because we don't know what our future is going to be. Her name is enough for you to know what problems lie before us."

"Her family, or yours?" I asked. "The antagonists?"

"Look around you," he waved a hand. "Almost everyone and their dog are eager antagonists in a Hindu-Muslim love story."

"I am not," I said defiantly.

"Just need an army of your clones, then," he laughed. "And we will be sorted. Anyway, why did I bring this up? It was not to tell you a sob story. It was to tell our friend Sameer that relationships take time to build, and even longer to sustain. The first step to both is to have faith."

Sameer drew sharply on his burning cigarette and exhaled a cloud. "You keep your faith. I will keep my disgruntlement."

"Cynic!" I muttered.

"Isn't he?" Swapnil agreed. "Hear it from Lover Boy himself. Before our next visit here, he will have scored his first date with Ruchi Karwal."

"Date?" I smirked. "Far out! Just because I thought she was very pretty, you can't assume I am pursuing her."

"Sameer is a cynic," said Aryan. "And you are a denialist."

"I am honest," I said.

"I believe him," said Sameer slowly, waiting for everyone to look at him, beseeching him to tell us why he believed me. "He is not pursuing her. I don't know Nakul to be the kind who'd pursue two ladies at a time."

I had half-seen this coming. I had seen the look of suspicion he wore on previous occasions when I hung out with Naina. The *I know where this is going* vibe I had been unable to detect accurately. But now, I knew. "Careful, there. For you know not what you are saying."

"Neither do we," said a confused Aryan.

"Nakul knows what I am saying," Sameer grinned. "That will be enough."

"Naina?" Swapnil guessed.

I slipped out of the booth. "You guys are crazy. There is a difference between being in love with someone and caring for a friend or going the extra mile for them."

"Never seen you going the extra mile for us, mate." Sameer stared at me, standing his ground. "I thought we were friends too!"

"I expected more maturity from a twenty-two-year-old," I said. "My bad. I am out of here." "Why are you getting so riled up?" Aryan tried to stop me. "It was just a question. If there is nothing to it, just say so and we will believe you."

"I am getting riled up because it is an absurd thought." My voice was shaky. "Naina – I have never thought of Naina like that."

"Fair point," said Aryan. "But not a very absurd thought either, if it crossed one's mind at all. Great friends can progress to better things."

"As far as Naina is concerned," I said, raising a hand, "being great friends is better than anything else it can be. I want it to stay that way. And I want you guys to understand."

"Then you don't need to get so agitated," said Sameer. "A bit rich coming from the guy who was once lecturing me on handling my relationship with Soha."

"Because there is a difference between the two," I snubbed in response. "Now don't get me started."

I took my seat again, although I was not getting a good feeling about letting this hangout extend to another round of drinks. Too much honesty between friends could be a huge cross to bear.

For a moment, it appeared Sameer had mellowed. "I am sorry if I crossed a line. I am glad to know you don't think that way about Naina. It is just that amongst all of us, we know you two are the closest. Hence, be careful. Your friend has found new friends."

"That does not bother me," I lied again.

"Your sullen face on the morning after the flood told me otherwise," he shrugged. "But I will take it if you say so. As it is, no point bothering about a friend who can move on so easily."

Aryan butted in, sensing the tension that was building up. "Guys, take it easy now. Change the subject."

But the shots had been fired. "Your opinions about people are so flaky, Sameer," I said. "Get a grip on yourself. I don't need a sermon on what friends I need to bother about. Surely not from someone who could not handle his own…"

Swapnil kicked me in the shin two seconds too late. Sameer's eyes scrunched, containing their tears. The clamour in the pub died amidst the painful moment of silence that clouded over our table.

"Thanks for reminding me, Nakul," Sameer spoke thickly. "You did go the extra mile for me, after all."

Nobody said another word that night. We split the bill and we split paths as we hurtled into an anti-climax to what was an ordinary, beautiful evening between four friends.

22

Our motivation to study for the fifth-trimester exams was at an all-time low. And for good reason. The CGPA had been cut-off until the fourth trimester. Our resumes had been packaged and packed off to the Placement Committee. Nothing that we would now do, or not do, in the fifth and sixth trimesters, would significantly alter our fate at Placements.

"As long as your boat does not capsize," the staff had warned. "So at the very least, ensure you don't score an F."

Add to that the size of the *Brand Building* guidebook I was reading, and I had every reason to question my hard work at the cost of zero return.

I sprawled on my bed with a big yawn. "This is boring. I am off for a walk. Will you join?"

Swapnil lay on his belly, his eyes dug into his books; his legs, anchored at the knees, swivelled back and forth like the pivots of a cross-trainer. "I will pass."

"Of course, you will pass," I said. "You will top the exams. Now let's go."

"I mean a raincheck," he grinned. "No walk for me. You seem out of sorts."

"I am," I admitted. "Any news from Sameer?"

His legs stopped dangling. He hung his head low; his right hand swept back towards his crown a thick tuft of hair that now covered his pensive eyes. "Let sleeping dogs lie. Give him – and yourself - some time to get over what happened at the pub."

"Was I wrong?" "Not my place to comment," he replied. In a gesture of abandoning this topic, his legs swivelled again.

I walked to the beach seeking a reprieve. The time was nudging noon. The sun was a scorcher. A gush of wind blew over the Arabian Sea and fanned the sweat running down my neck. The dry sand was hot enough to fry my bottom, therefore I chose to walk along the tide instead. The seaside at this odd hour was relatively desolate, save for a bunch of children playing cricket not too far away. From a distance, I sensed a commotion as the group distanced itself from one child. He was a year or two younger than the rest. Twirling a bat in the sand, he looked downward in despondence as an impromptu committee was formed before him. Heads shook in disapproval and they motioned for him to walk away from the boundary line that had been formed by shoes and slippers placed equidistantly in a concentric circle.

Feeling an instant connection with his situation, I ambled over to the boy so I could take a closer look. I had expected him to be sullen from the rejection. Instead, he had cheerfully strayed away from the other kids and had busied himself with a tennis ball he had in his possession. Repetitively, he hurled it up in the air and followed its trajectory before catching it in his boyish hands.

I looked at his bat. A shining piece of willow recently oiled and knocked in. A bright red *Brittania* label adorned its centre. "Nice bat."

He looked at me for a second, then continued offering himself catching practice. "I got it from my parents as a birthday gift."

"When was it?" I asked, presuming it could not be today. Ostracization from a cricket team on one's birthday sounded incongruous with the ways of the world.

But then he enlightened me. "Today."

I felt my heart sink as I wished him a happy birthday. "Why won't those boys play with you?"

Shamefacedly, he swung imaginary shots with his bat as he explained. "They say I am not good enough. I drop a lot of catches."

"That was me as a child," I smiled. "I dropped way more catches than I caught. But aren't those boys a little older than you?"

"We are all neighbours," he said. "Our families always get us all to play together. Except now, because I am not playing."

"Can I play with you?" I asked on impulse. I had lost all desire to play cricket many moons ago. But picking it up again did not seem like a big ask of myself if it brought even a sliver of joy to the birthday boy." "Sure," he quipped and tossed the ball in my hand before marching twenty-two yards to take a stance with his bat.

"So, it is decided that I bowl," I muttered to myself. "Ok, be ready for my beamers."

My deliveries were hardly legitimate, far less were they beamers. But after a dozen painful swings of the arm, I got around to bowling straight, simplistic ones that he drove, punched, cut and pulled with fair ease. In ten minutes, I realised that standing in for ten other fielders was not a fantastic idea given my sub-optimal fitness levels. By the eleventh minute, I was sweating like a monkey and panting like a dog.

"That is it," I said, holding the sides of my waist and sinking my knees in the sand. "I am beaten. Are you going to feed me a birthday cake for all my effort or what?"

He smiled shyly. "Yeah."

"Surely you have a party on," I guessed.

"I have one at home," he said.

"Are these dolts invited?" I asked, pointing at the other boys.

The smile was replaced by a frown of repulsion. "Yes. But I have other friends coming too. So I don't really care."

"You are a popular guy!" I marvelled.

"Daddy just tells me we need to make as many friends as we can," he spoke slowly, as though the advice had been committed to memory by frequent repetition. "*If you run out of some, you should always have some others to bank on.*"

As I walked back to the hostel later that afternoon, I carried with me the worldly wisdom of the boy's father. Easy, simple words that should have felt easy to implement. And yet, I found, friends were more like collagen than like cookies. Replenishment with new pieces was easier said than done.

23

Ruchi's sea-deep eyes had the power to spark off a second Trojan war. Her beauty inspired thoughtful poetry. But I could not indulge myself in it because a fat textbook of Operations Management lay in her manicured hands and that did not make for a very poetic setting.

"Are you sure it is a good time?" She asked. "You appear a little distracted."

I drew my gaze away, just in case. Appreciating good looks always needs to follow the three-second rule. Cometh the fourth second, you are being plain rude and lecherous. "Just a little sleep deprived, that's it. But yes, yes, of course, it is a good time."

In some past moment of braggadocio, I had told her I had scored an 'A' in Operations Management. It was no feat worth boasting about unless it was the *only* subject in which one ever scored an 'A', which was the case, and therefore here we were.

"Chapter 8, Page 134," she said to stir me out of my stupor.

I flipped the pages with trembling fingers, perfectly conscious of the company I was seated in but also because there was a looming restiveness inside of me. The buzz around Placements Week had been giving me sharp bouts of acidity. And true to my standards of rising to danger only at the last minute, I had started to feel strange pangs of career-related anxiety. As though MBA was a large vessel I had hopped on to before learning of its imminent capsize.

But even beyond Placements, there was a restlessness to snatch and pocket every little remaining moment that was worth treasuring at this place. To let the odd grouse slide, to take pictures that would be revisited when I missed these people and their lame jokes, to write each other parting notes of wisdom or even complaints. As the months to convocation reduced, the campus had started feeling like a guest house due to be checked out of. It was foolhardy of emotional idiots like me to ever imagine this day was not to come. Against this desperate struggle to clutch at straws, friends had got busier in their pursuit of the Big Placement Week. The group hangouts were far and few. Feelings and fears were seldom shared. And this made the paucity of time starker.

I fumbled through the pages until I reached Page 134. "Did I really score an A in this?"

She laughed. "Humblebrag!"

While I loved that I could make her laugh – she had lovely laughter – it was hardly funny. I wish I could tell her I had every honest intention to help her. But I needed to help myself first. Just then, the screen of my laptop fired up a message from Aryan, over the local chat messenger.

Do you believe in the adage "Failure is the first step to success?"

Yes. Why?

Congrats. We have just taken the first step. The results of the agri-business contest are out. And we have failed to qualify.

I slammed the screen shut. Admitting to one's failures did not fit within the metrics of humblebrag. "I am so sorry. I will have to stand you up."

"Go for it." She placed her hand on mine in reassurance. "You seem a bit…beside yourself."

I ran out like a headless chook looking for Aryan. I found him finally in the café, munching on a very leafy sandwich as though celebrating the verdict of the news he had just shared with me. "Partner! Come hither. Help me chalk out our next plan of action!"

"Do you think this is funny?" I asked, agitated.

"Do you have an option but to laugh it off?" he asked.

"That won't solve the problem, laughing it off," I replied. "We are running out of time and I am feeling totally…"

"Worthless?" he guessed.

"Thank you!" I snarled. "But yes. Worthless."

He motioned me to take a chair. "We have two more contests lined up. Our final shots, but let us give them our everything. One is a Case Study on *Diva Touch*. The other is an ad-film competition. All hope is not lost."

I rubbed my hands over my face like it was a magic lamp that would sweat out a genie who would grant me a wish or two. When no genie appeared, I pushed back the chair and rose to leave. "I am giving up. Maybe I should not have been here in the first place."

"Nakul!" He barricaded my exit with the biceps he was very proud of. "If you should not have been here, neither should have several others. You are not as bad as you think. And you really need to build a lot more self-confidence than that if you've got to brave Placement Week."

"Sign up for the competitions," I relented. "I am in. But I don't feel like a pep talk right now."

But he gave me a pep talk anyway. Tirelessly, sincerely, methodically. He reminded me of his own strife as he tried to gain his father's love and trust. Of the family, he had found in me. Then he proceeded to tell me that he and I were like the buffalo and the fly in a symbiotic relationship, at which point I asked him to stop and assured him I was completely remotivated. We sat days and nights at the end in the library, prepared for the two competitions, studied for our exams, and took only the occasional tea break at Govind's. When the week of submissions arrived, we were satisfied with our effort and more importantly, with whatever experience we had assimilated while preparing for the submissions. The Goliath of Placements felt a little less difficult to vanquish.

After a gap of several weeks, we took to the terrace that night. The others were still MIA, but we made do with two for company. There was a nip in the air. The sky was a dark starless sheet. From the ground floor downstairs, music blared off expensive loudspeakers amidst the chatter of joyous teenagers.

"What a fine age," I sighed. "Life is one big party with nothing to worry about. How I miss those days!"

"Stop whining!" he said. "Your life here has been one big party too. And you are a couple of years older than those kids. Or has two weeks of library time aged you by twenty years already?" He waited for me to respond; when I did not, he added. "This is just the fear of the unknown talking. Relax. Our careers will chart the course they deserve, even without us fretting about it. I know I was fretting about it not long ago. But I had an epiphany."

Career. How could I not fret about it? The word had been drilled into my conscience since the day I started school. It was uttered with joy when I excelled in an exam, with concern at dinnertime when I sought to go out on picnics with friends, and with rage when I was found missing from my study room a night ahead of exams. From primary to secondary to high school boards, the word graduated from being aspirational to being a phantom. In the four years of Engineering, I heard little of it because almost all hope had been lost in the Kapoor household about my 'career.' Then the MBA option appeared like a life vest. Someone said I should take the CAT and squeeze into a B-school; then all the mistakes of B-Tech could be undone. Now, here I was. I knew I had a career alright. There was some job I'd get. Something that could be talked about in my family's social circles. Beyond that essential checkbox, I had ticked nothing. I did not know what company, what sector, or what role I wanted.

"FMCG will pack me off to the hinterlands," I started slowly. "Banking is not my cup of tea. Should I try IT?"

"After majoring in Marketing?" he laughed. "Yeah, that will be a disruptive breakthrough you could be proud of."

"If only I qualify," I said.

"Try the Gaming industry," he said. "Remember the days of the first trimester when we always took to the last row so we could play Mario Brothers on our laptops?"

Mario Brothers, sigh. The single biggest contributor to our survival in the first trimester was when we understood nothing except that we had to record close to a hundred per cent attendance. Now that I looked back at it, my life was like Mario's. My princess was the dream job I needed to land. The pressure of assignments and exams, the dejection following bad grades was the oompa loompa I needed to fight. Placement Week was the dragon spewing fireballs at me right in front of the finish line. The only difference was that, unlike Mario, I was not being granted three lives to get the princess.

24

"Hey, you there! Last bench!"

"Sleepyhead. Last bench!"

The words fell on my ears lighter than the flying chalk did on my head. I woke with a start.

Vandana elbowed me, uttering the faintest whisper. "He heard you snore."

Through red and puffy eyes, I stared into the Professor's hawk eyes as he stared at me from the other end of the classroom. I wanted to compliment him for his great aim with the chalk. Even at that age, he knew precision.

"What did I just say?" he asked.

I winced. Why did a student always have to retell the teacher what he just said? It showed an utter lack of conviction on the teacher's end. Tch. Hardly inspiring. I squinted to read his terrible handwriting – between a cricket fielder and a calligraphist I could tell what he was better at – and I understood zilch.

"Singing lullabies, are we?" he roared.

How I wish. After weeks of long nights pulled over the competitions, I really could afford a good morning's sleep in the airconditioned classroom.

As the Professor would proceed to explain, my struggles had got nothing on the ones he had endured *when he was my age*. "When I was your age, I was a Sales Representative in Eastern UP. I travelled ticketless in the engine room of slow trains in hot summers to get to my job. That sweat and toil are what has got me here. Do you aspire to my position? Answer me!"

There was only one politically correct answer to that question, and it did not have room to include a question as to why he travelled ticketless. "Absolutely do, Sir."

After a long pause, his sermon ended in an abrupt anti-climax. "Then stay awake!"

When he returned to face the blackboard, Vandana leaned into me and whispered again. "Hard to stay up?"

I nodded.

"I can tell," she said. "Your eyes are ripe red cherries. Can I help?"

"Help keep me awake."

"Should I talk dirty to you?" she asked and giggled at her own joke.

I returned a look of horror and disbelief. "Gosh, how much you have changed in two years!"

She grinned. For a moment it appeared we had caught the Professor's attention again. She ducked her head and spoke. "Was just kidding, bozo. You are not that lucky anyway. Here!"

She pulled out a notepad and scribbled on it before pushing it towards me.

Let's write and talk. I won't let you fall asleep again in class.

Lifesaver. I was working late into the night.

How unusual! Also, what's up with you? Haven't seen you around for days.

I could say the same about all of you.

I miss the gang that once hung out with.

Do you?

What do you mean? You don't?

Is it worth it?

Nothing.

No. Tell me. You are being weird.

I just wonder if it is worth it. This game of false expectations.

Who hurt you? Let me go smack that person now.

Scratch that. Tell me something nice.

Evening plan at Alfredo's. Naina is going with the Finnies. She asked me to come along. And then she asked me to ask you.

I read the message with careful consideration. Then I tore the piece of paper off the notebook and folded it, stuffed it into my shirt pocket. Something told me these little conversations would make for fine souvenirs later.

"REALLY weird!" She rolled her eyes.

As we walked out at the end of the session, she pulled me by the arm. "Weirdo! I asked you a question. Dinner at Alfredo's.'

"I am not invited," I said dryly.

"You are!" She laughed again. Something in her laughter told me she knew what I was hinting at. But she was trying her best to skirt the subject. For my sake. "She asked me to invite you."

"So, now there is a conduit between me and her," I said.

She cajoled me, pushing me gently through the door. "Don't be like that, man. Don't dissect the matter so much. I am going. Does that count for nothing?"

I stopped to gauge her earnestness. "Ok, fine. We will go."

What a terrible mistake that turned out to be. I was at Alfredo's at the appointed time. The others arrived half an hour later, sauntering together in a group. Barring Naina and Vandana there were four others – three boys and a girl – her *Finnies*. The introductions were quick and formal. But once we took seats at the circular table of the restaurant, the distance across the table and the loud music provided the perfect stage for the newfound friends to form little pockets of their own private conversations and giggles. Naina could call me a child all she liked, but when you end up being the only sidelined diner at a table for seven, you have every reason to throw a childish, hissy fit.

I exchanged looks with Vandana, who was the only one who read my discomfort.

I am sorry I brought you into this, she seemed to say.

You don't need to be sorry. Especially when those who should be, hardly are.

As if on cue, Naina looked up from the closed-loop laughathon she was in and asked me. "Why so glum, chum?"

"Not glum!" I smiled a fake smile that was meant to be a smirk. "Having the time of my life."

The sarcasm was either lost on her, or she chose not to heed it. The ordeal at this table was getting impossible to bear. It did not help that the service was slow too. Luckily, my phone rang, allowing me to excuse myself from this very awkward moment.

"Yes, Aryan?" I answered after stepping out.

His voice was a lot more serious than usual. "Dude. The results of *Diva Touch* are out."

"And we have not made it?" I pre-empted.

"I have," he explained slowly and then stopped.

It took me some time to register. Industrious friends leaving you behind in the race for grades had taken some getting used to. Now the only friend who had given me company in the category of laggards had suddenly let go.

That awkward moment when you need to feel delighted for your friend but all you can feel is disappointment and betrayal. "That…that is wonderful! I am happy for you, mate."

"We still have that ad-film." He knew what I was going through.

"Listen, don't worry," I told him. "Focus on your Finals. I am going to be ok."

I walked back to the dinner table with even lesser resolve to stick around. "Something has come up."

Vandana rose from her seat. Naina rose her gaze. The others behaved as though I did not exist.

"What is the matter?" Naina asked. "You look upset."

Breaking news. Yes, I was. Would this question be followed by another question or an offer of support? Let us see. "Yes. I am."

She did offer pity and platitudes, I had to give her that. "Take care, *yaar*. I will call you later tonight, ok? Let's catch up."

Well, what do I say then? Thanks for the advice, I guess. Boys don't cry. Hence, I did not. But Vandana did notice the moist eyes as she saw me walk out.

"Hey!" She came running outside. "I am sorry."

I shrugged, looking sideways so the tears could roll right back into their sockets. "What for?"

"I should not have asked you to come," she admitted.

"Go back inside, Vandana," I said. "It is not your fault. You don't have to apologise on behalf of others. This goodness will make me sick."

Instead, she stepped forward and hugged me. All that I needed at the moment. Yet, this stupid heart longed for the hug it was not meant to get. "I don't want to ask you right now. Meet me in the evening and tell me what is bothering you."

I felt like a prick saying this, but my disillusionment was past my control. I drew back gently. "Never mind it."

As I sat in the nearest autorickshaw, I heard her call out again. "Whether or not you come, I will be waiting at the quadrangle at eleven tonight."

25

A dozen young executives in black business suits are seated in a large conference room of the head office, waiting for the chief to arrive. I walk in and occupy the chair at the centre.

"We are here today to discuss Bouquet," I say, "the new mid-segment women's perfume we intend to launch next month. We need to get on with the communication plan for the product across all major metros first. I need ideas from the team regarding the approach. May I suggest we begin with a teaser campaign for the first fortnight..."

I hear a commotion amongst three executives at one corner of the table. They hush-hush amongst each other in a huddle.

"Gentlemen, let yourselves be heard," I say affirmatively. "We are all a part of this."

They don't heed my warning. Instead, others at the table join the covert debate. I lose my patience after a few repeated warnings. Exasperated, I slam my fist on the table.

"You bloody louts! Where have you come from? Do you realise there is such a thing as boardroom etiquette?"

"Pardon me, Nakul," one of them retorts. "But after due deliberation, we have realised we need to leave certain decisions to ourselves. So, spare us the lecture. We shall be quite comfortable handling this on our own."

"I am your boss!" I shout back.

"We couldn't care less," Another replies. "You have been no good of late. See what you did to Diva Touch! I feel sorry to say this, but you are a failure…"

A nap at the odd hour of after evening but before bedtime never did one's mental health any good. I woke up feeling like trash. My breath smelt like a pit of compost manure. My legs, as though tied to boulders, refused to plod. A copy of the *Business Standards* fluttered on the edge of my bed under the gust of the ceiling fan. Gerard Tellis, the renowned economist, was on the cover. Below his beaming smile, a caption: *Do you have what it takes?*

I turned the magazine upside down and dragged myself to the bathroom. I ran a toothbrush through the length and breadth of my aching mouth, scrubbed myself, and combed my hair for longer than usual just in a bid to buy more time before having to inevitably step out. Vandana would have it no other way and I would hate myself if I stood her up. For if I did, what would be the difference…

She waited in the thinly occupied quadrangle of our college; her laptop played soft music as she fervently worked on a caselet. A table afar had a jamming session on; Atif's *Woh Lamhe* played in the aching foretelling of moments that would soon become Past Tense. Disdainful of the activity happening around her, Silky, the stray black cat that had found its way onto campus years ago and had since been lovingly accepted, sulked in a corner and licked her hips to keep herself amused.

"I thought you would not come," she waved, shutting her laptop screen down.

"And still *you* came?" I sank into the seat next to hers. "Why did you have to be nice?"

She clucked with a cringe. "See, you put ordinary acts of friendship on a pedestal. Exaggerate them in your head. This is what causes you all the hurt. There is nothing *nice* about what I did. It is just what friends do."

"And yet," I rued, "sometimes they don't."

The words stayed with her; crossing her arms, she leaned back, looking away with a frown. Carefully measuring the words escaping her mouth, she lingered. "I was just as uncomfortable at dinner as you were."

"Why?" It was more an accusation than a question. "They were your friends."

The niceness peeled a tiny bit to convey contempt. "So you think, isn't it? Because you have not asked. I know none of the Finnies myself. I have hung out with them a few times because Naina tagged me along. But I am not in on their jokes, their inner-circle discussions, several of their plans."

"But you have hung out before." I was adamant. My awkwardness was worse than hers.

"At her insistence," she said. "Because, as I said, that's what friends do."

"Turns out," I said sourly, "friends also do what she does. What do you do then?"

She stuttered; taking her time to choose between sympathy and admonishment, she spoke. "You are letting her behaviour, her choices, consume you. Don't be this person, Nakul. You can do better. Yes, you have been there for her. She has told me so. But if you are not getting the reciprocation from her – and if reciprocation is indeed what you need – then you have the easy option of steering clear."

I had a ready rebuttal to offer. A counter-argument to every sane advice she offered. However, I found myself incapable of speaking any further. A sense of fatigue drew me into a lull as I crouched on the chair, crushed by the weight of my expectations from others.

What's up, Buster! The Voice was back to haunt me.

There you are again. Not another sermon, please.

Feeling the doldrums, Nakul? Life's thrown you a raw deal? People are being unkind to you? Aww, you poor baby!

Here comes another sage telling me I am being a child.

No, you are an idiot. You spend two decades of your life in the protective cocoon of your family. Waste your precious two years here doing absolutely nothing. And when you feel you are in the pits, you totter around your friends asking them for a healing touch! What an idiot!

What is unreasonable in my ask? Did I not…

Oh, you did alright, you emotional fool. You did. What you did was your wish. What others are doing, or not doing, is their wish. No matter how many Sameers and Vandanas talk you out of your incessant wallowing in self-pity, you will never understand. You will always stay stuck in the swamp, blinded to the rope you can use to wade out. Just because you are looking for that hand that will stretch out in an offer of help.

Untrue.

Yes, true. Because I know even now as Vandana is wasting her time trying to cheer you up, your eye is drifting towards your watch. Because Naina told you she will call you tonight, and you are wondering when that precious phone call will eventuate.

I am going to get out of the swamp.

Be good for you if you do. Because as I said before: in the end when you look around, you will see you are all alone.

"The cat's got your tongue!" She shook me by my knee, waking me from my daze.

I adjusted my eyes, smarting under the blinding lamp that shone overhead. "I won't be that person, Vandana. I can do better, yes."

"You had better," she said. Ponderously, she asked me a question. "You are not in love with her, are you?"

"What, are you crazy!" The question was not outrageous or bizarre. I could imagine where it came from – the extra fondness for that one friend is always a blurred line. But in my head, I could never be clearer. The friendship was too sacred for me to be allowed to be replaced by anything else.

She agreed immediately. "I thought as much. All the more reason then that you need to let go of whatever is bothering you. Because as far as friends are concerned, the road does end at some point. If not now, it sure will when either of you finds a partner. Or do you think this joyride will chug along forever?"

She made a point I could not refute. Hence, I chose the easier option. "Now let us change the topic."

Even as I said that I couldn't help but notice the time of the night and then look at my phone which had still not rung. She regaled me with stories from her Nainital home. We talked about our shared yearning for a visit back to the families, and about the bittersweet memories we were leaving behind us in a flash. We strolled back to her hostel in the dead of the night, and it was only after dropping her as I walked back alone, my resolve went crumbling to pieces like a block of fetta. The laptop was in the hostel room which was still farther away. This could not wait. I made a detour back to the college and scampered up the stairs to enter the cyber café. The automatic lights came on as I swung the door open, as though questioning the arrival of a visitor at that ungodly hour. The computer took two minutes to fire up, during which time I weakly debated with myself the need for all this.

Only until the *Compose Email* button presented itself on the screen.

Dear Naina,

After ample thought, I have decided to write to you. Because for all other means to contact you, I need to make an appointment. Of late I have seen a chasm develop...

26

Urgent meeting for second-year students regarding the guidelines and instructions for Placement Week: New Auditorium, 3 PM

I broke into a sweat on reading the text on the noticeboard. The Day was almost here. The single answer to the countless times we had been asked *Why MBA?* since the time we had started preparing for our entrance exams and attending mock interviews to make it to The Ivy League. My grades had not done much for me. As a saving grace, Aryan and I had won the ad-making contest in Indore the previous week. Alas, a feat achieved too late to be put on my CV.

The auditorium was filled with the entire batch at the said time as everyone waited for Nilesh and Arvind, the heads of the Placement Committee, to take centre stage and tell us what the important meeting was about. They could have detailed the agenda on the noticeboard too, but then that would have diluted their sense of importance. So they made us wait fifteen minutes before showing up with exaggerated swag and fluorescent markers twirling in their fingers.

"Quiet, everyone!" Nilesh clapped his hands.

"The audacity!" Someone snarled in the audience.

But Nilesh had the skin of an elephant. He wore the comment as a compliment. "Yes. As you all know we have been burning the midnight oil, at the expense of our own preparation for interviews, to make Placement Week a roaring success for all of you."

Arvind, the milder of the two loudmouths, took the mic so that coming to the point would not appear to be such an ordeal after all. "The shortlisted CVs for three companies are out: International Confectioneries & Foods, Royal Westend Bank, and Home Solution Paints. These names will be put up on the noticeboard after this meeting. The others, please don't be disheartened. Just because you didn't make it to the top three does not mean you aren't getting a job. Hang in there."

"This meeting could have been an email!" Someone shouted again from the crowd.

"But there is another thing we need to talk to you about," said Nilesh. "And that is the boardroom etiquette we have to maintain in all Group Discussions and Interviews. Remember, upholding your institute's honour even in your testing times is the hallmark of…"

A huge commotion followed in the crowd. In front of the steaming red faces of Nilesh and Arvind, the crowd staged a walkout – no, a run-out – of the auditorium. Everyone deposited around the noticeboard like swarming bees around a beehive. The peon had to jostle his way through a hostile and restless crowd as he carefully pinned the printout of the shortlisted names on the noticeboard before bounding out of the people trapped in a tearing hurry.

I called out to Swapnil from the rear of the circle. "Swapnil, check for me too!"

Swapnil rose on his toes and, taking the support of nameless shoulders in front of him, jumped up a few times to go through the entire list. He made his way back to me with a grim expression. "Your name is not there."

I felt my breath go cold. "In which company?"

The discomfort with which he tried to respond was all I needed to know the answer. "All three."

"Sorry, what?"

"All three."

The next question was pointless. If Aryan had left my side in the Mission of Underachievers, Swapnil was far from being a contender. "And you?"

He simply nodded; he had no heart to spell it out for me.

"Ah, lovely!" I said. "Congratulations. I will be right back."

I dragged myself out of the lobby in the hope of fresh air. But like a long-awaited phone call that rings only when you are driving, Naina appeared out of the blue and struck me on the head in what might have been a friendly swat.

"Where the hell have you been all week?" She asked.

"Indore." I tried to walk away, but she kept pace.

"So I learnt," she said. "Congratulations on winning the contest!"

"Thank you...look," I looked up and closed my eyes. I couldn't believe I was still expending energy on this. "Let us talk later."

"Why?" She pursued. "And what was that rubbish email for?"

"Childish?" I stopped and turned back to glare at her. "Tell me. Was it childish?"

Carried away in the moment of tumult, I did not realise until I laid sight on heads turning and Naina retracting with shock and hurt, that I had crossed a line with my volume and tone. "Sorry."

But she was walking away already, and it was now I that had to keep pace. "Naina. I didn't mean to shout."

She let go of my hand and had an equal go at me. "Yes, CHILDISH! Because it will take you an entire lifetime to realise you are trying to make me the person that you are, and chalk is never going to become cheese. I cared for you, Nakul. Maybe I still do. But I am done trying to explain myself to you."

"Oh, that tripe again!" My tone was now subdued. But my dismay would just not ebb. "*Oh, Nakul! I care for you, this friendship is so special, but my way of expressing it is different...blah, blah, and more blah!*"

There was a shiver in her voice. "That you should mock me for saying that is all I needed to know about you today. You are pathetic, Nakul. Go drop this boulder of expectations on someone else. I did not ever ask you to go the extra mile for me. I never asked for your exclusive time. I did not ask you to go be a hero in front of the Dean for me. All your choices. I am not going to apologise for things I have not done."

"This is it, then," I said. It was a question, a prompt for her to convince me otherwise.

She converted it into a definitive statement. "Sure is."

Rubbing salt into many a wound, Nilesh snuck up on me like a bad omen, seconds after she walked away. "Buddy! Where did you get shortlisted?"

Fucking rascal. I was sure he had checked the list, ensured I was not on it and then decided to come ask me just so he could hear it from me. "Nowhere."

"NOT EVEN ONE of the three?" His eyes had the hunger of a despicable sadist.

I plastered on a smile. "Yeah, that's what *nowhere* usually means."

"How come?"

"You ask lovely questions, Nilesh," I said. "I wish you could conduct my interview, whenever that happens. Now if you don't mind, I have somewhere to go die."

I headed back to the hostel to hide from the world. As I turned into a lane that connected two rows of expensive bungalows owned by high-flying investment bankers and film stars, I came across a huge, stinky heap of rot comprising stale vegetables, decaying fruits, and unfinished gravies that had been thrown out of the windows of these expensive bungalows. Atop this mound sat a wiry, old man with both arms chopped off at their elbows. His skin was wrinkled and scarred by wounds that appeared decades old. The lines that contoured his senile face, and his sunken eyes, betrayed the unrevealed saga of his life. Incongruously, the man himself appeared calm as he sat cross-legged and, much to my horror, sank his mouth into the rot to devour the grotesque remains of what might have been someone's food from the previous night. Unmindful of the fibre that stuck to his eyebrows and scraggly beard, he chewed with contentment. Upon swallowing the last bit of his morsel, he prepared to stoop again when I went running across the street to stop him.

"Wait!" I said, fumbling for a packet of biscuits I had kept in my bag that morning before forgetting to eat them amidst all that had transpired. "Have these instead."

He offered a limp smile as I placed the packet beneath the pile he was perched on. Realising the gaffe when he motioned towards his elbows, I opened the packet with trembling hands and lay the biscuits open. He nodded in gratitude; I gathered he was too hungry to speak. Sliding down the filth he was on, he now settled next to it and scooped down on the biscuits.

I continued onward to the hostel with yet another reminder that I had enough to be grateful for and cribbing about the have-nots was not good form. Eye-openers rarely worked a permanent charm; however, if this episode could help lift my spirits until I landed a job and got over the line, I'd take it. Sprinting up the stairs to the third floor, I retreated on an impulse and walked back to the second floor and rapped the door of Room 204.

Sameer answered it; his spectacles fogged and overworked, and a pen dangled from his mouth. "Oye. Come on in."

The room was a shocker for a parent who might have walked in on that mess. But for a pair of eyes that was accustomed to Swapnil's unbeatable levels of disorderliness, this place felt like a monastery. "I need to apologise."

He swept a hand over his bed, taking down with it at least three books, one USB drive, and two empty packets of potato chips. "Sit. And go ahead."

"What?"

"Apologise," he grinned.

"Ok. I am sorry for what I said the other night," I said.

"It's ok, buddy. I am sorry too," he admitted. "I crossed a line myself. I was so wrong with what I said about Naina."

His voice was coated thick with observation when he saw me look up at him. "Is something wrong?"

I shook my head. "Just some bitter almonds I chewed on."

He understood. "Say no more. We have bigger fish to fry right now. Let's go for a walk and clear our heads, what say?"

27

On the eleventh day of the Year 2006, the hostel was a large pup tent housing over a hundred restless young men preparing for war. The smell of freshly starched business suits coasted along the corridors. Bottles of cologne, shaving foam and hair gel were being tossed across rooms and shared between friends. The use of the toilet was in overdrive because anxious brains had little control over their rumbling bellies. Frequently from the ground floor, someone would bellow an instruction:

Attention. The panel from XYZ Company is reaching campus in thirty minutes. Shortlisted candidates need to get there NOW.

And the hundred bodies in their fragrant starched suits would run helter-skelter, fussing about.

In stark contrast to the frenzy around him, Swapnil lay asleep in his bed like a baby, snuggled up in a blanket that he had last washed never. The previous day – labelled 'Day Zero' – saw some of the most coveted organisations scoop up the cream of the batch, offering them handsome salaries and fancy job titles. Swapnil was the cream of the cream, the first to get picked by Home Solution Paints. On the night of Day Zero when the batch hurled three cheers at him and the others, he politely subdued the noise by telling them the partying would wait until everyone was placed. He then sat with the rest of us, preparing us for the next day's onslaught.

When I awoke on this morning of 'Day One', I found my suit lying on my bed, picked up by him the previous night from the dry cleaner. And an SMS on my phone: *I will likely be asleep when you will be off. All the best. I will join you on campus soon so we can celebrate together.*

If I could choose to be someone else, I would be a Swapnil. A gentleman, a worker bee, a true friend, and a bloody batch topper who ran home with the finest job. Did this man have anything going wrong in his life, I nearly asked myself before remembering his story about Nazneen & Two Pugnacious Families.

The door swung open. Aryan stood donning his grey blazer, blowing air into his hands to keep them warm. "Let's go?"

I circled a finger over his white face. "Did you just see a ghost?"

"I am nervous!" He answered jumpily. "Don't ask me stupid questions. Let's go."

"What for?" I asked. "Our names haven't been shortlisted on any company for today yet."

"Some of the shortlists will be rolled out on a live projector through the day," he said impatiently. "I don't know about you. But I can't sit here guessing."

I picked myself up and accompanied him to where all the action was happening. "Ok, can you at least stop flitting about like a moth? What happened to all your conviction that *we will rock*?"

"I was wrong!" He squeaked. "Ok? I am only human. The conviction was what it was – mere words. They hold no good before the moment of truth."

His anxiety was only exacerbated once we got off the rickshaw to see a red carpet rolled out at the entrance. Students from the junior batch stood at the gate with bouquets, waiting for various company executives to arrive. "Why do they have to do this? The extravagance is only going to kill me."

I stopped him and held him by both shoulders. "You are triggering me also. Stop. Take a deep breath, close your eyes, and walk with me to the library. You can do this. Imagine we are just going to play a game of Counterstrike."

He inhaled sharply; closing his eyes, he nodded. "Counterstrike."

Ruchi Karwal stood in the hallway. A Volunteer lanyard hung around her neck; she smiled on seeing me. "You still need to teach me Operations Management."

I felt the cold rush of restlessness in my ears even as I tried my best to stay calm. "Still due."

She extended a hand. "Nail your interview today. Then teach me."

I thanked her and prepared to leave; ten feet away Aryan had stopped, glaring at me irately as I chose to live a romantic moment in a time of crisis. "Hey, listen," I said to her. "After all this madness ends, you know – do you like good coffee?"

She clenched her jaws to keep from breaking into a laugh as I beat around the bush. "Prithvi Café serves some wonderful coffee in case you'd like to try it."

"Are you asking me out?" She tore into laughter. "Hey, a tip. When you go in for an interview, be a little more direct than this when making a point!"

"So is it a yes?" I asked hopefully.

Her infectious chuckle made me forget, even if for a second, what I was here for. "They aren't giving you a job after just one question, right? There will be more questions asked, Nakul, before you hear a *yes*!"

Walking backwards so I could take another lasting look, I said. "I will come prepared."

Aryan was a steaming hotpot by the time I reached him. "Why hello, Romeo! Remember me?"

I used my palms for blinders. "Alright now, intense focus. I promise."

Oh my God. This library, this dear old library was once home to our daylong endeavours of being the newest Counterstrike champions and to several late-night romantic rendezvouses in its nooks and crannies. Tonight, it looked like the abattoir I had once crossed in Juhu Gully. Only, the one hundred and seventy-five chickens here wore starched business suits, were too nervous to even cluck, and had put on several layers of perfume because nobody bathes during Placement Week. Yes, this is a tacit rule. If someone claims to have showered during this week, they are either untrustworthy or had not been exposed to the esoteric cure to our anxiety that Govind, along with his sugary, creamy tea, gave us a month before our big day. "DO NOT BATHE FOR SEVEN DAYS AHEAD OF GETTING A JOB."

"But how will we know what day we are going to land a job?" We had asked, circling him like followers beseeching their sage to dispense pearls of wisdom.

Expertly pouring equal amounts of tea into ten cups, he had smiled. "Faith. It will tell you."

Here we were now. Two days in, stinking AND still jobless. *Thank you for nothing, Govind.*

"Get me the CVs of the marketing batch. Now." Nilesh squealed into his walkie-talkie. Then, casting a glance at us so caustic that it could have burnt us if not for the air conditioner, he barked into it again. "Just the leftovers, I mean. Not the entire batch."

The leftovers. The outcasts. The nobodies who could not dance to Sukhbir's *O Ho Ho Ho* on the quadrangle the previous night because they did not have an offer letter yet. The ones who kept getting patted on the shoulder were told that it would all be ok because "after all, there will be something out there for you."

"You will be fine, Nakul." Nilesh put his walkie-talkie aside and hugged me. His affectation reached me even if his warmth did not. "Just don't be nervous."

Yes, easier said than done for the bloke who landed a 12L package with American Money Corporation on Day 0 and then marched the length and breadth of the campus to ensure that all two hundred and forty students as well as Silky, the stray cat that had merely snarled at us from a corner of the quad for two years, knew how much he would be earning three months from now.

"Bytesphere should be on campus any moment now. And trust me, they hire by the dozen. You are sure to get in there."

"Thanks, bro," I replied, deadpan and beat. "That does my confidence a world of good."

Bloody Prick took it as a compliment. Not that I expected better from him. When I had scored a 2.86 GPA in the first trimester, he had followed me to the loo only to tell me that Professor Wankhede had reckoned nobody in the history of this institute had ever scored a 2.86. I had vowed that very evening as waste fluids escaped my raging body, I would raze Nilesh's arrogance to the ground. Like many other vows and dreams, this one had been razed to the ground too. If I had leisure time at hand right now, I'd take to a corner, mull over the twenty-one months I had wasted here, and undo some serious errors of judgement. Not least of those would be heeding Aryan's advice that it was only street-smartness, and not grades, that were going to propel our careers.

Flash Consumer Durables have now arrived on campus. The giant projector facing us came alive. A hush of excitement rose in the room as people clutched onto yet another straw of hope.

"Are you game for Flash?" Aryan asked me. In the recesses of his mouth was a Happydent that had been working in overdrive to calm his nerves.

I circled my whitened face with my index finger. "What does this tell you? Do I look like I call the shots?"

"It is the attitude…" he began but stopped soon as he saw my jaw drop.

"You – really, no really, Aryan," I shook my head in disbelief. "Even now you won't stop. So, anyway. Yes, I am game for Flash, Aryan. Do you think Flash is game for me?"

We stood with bated breath as another verdict unfolded before us. The cursor inched painfully to the right with each character in each name being typed.

"Why is the bloody thing so slow?" hissed Aryan.

"Slow tease," I said.

Abhinav Chopra

Rahul Mehta

Nandini Tagde

Aryan Nair

"Yes!" I clapped in excitement. "Yes, you made it!"

"Hush!" He quietened me. "It is still rolling."

Salil Gaur

N...

"That's you! That's you!" He dug his nails into my chunky arm.

Something told me that now just because he had said it, this was not meant to be my name. Because except for the ad-making competition, nothing that he had assured me about in two years had actually materialised. But the ticking cursor did shoot up my pulse rate.

Niraj Kaul

I stared at the screen with a dropped jaw, like a pug waiting to be offered a biscuit. Until the ticker finally appeared: *Congratulations and wish you all the best.*

"So, that's that," I said and then shook my head like a turbine on noting his look of sympathy. "No, no, no. Say nothing, please. It will only make things worse for me. Do you know what will help? Go up there and crack it! Show me the path."

He handed me a fist bump and darted. I sat sulking in a corner of the library, wondering if it was the temperature of the air conditioner or just my disquiet sending shivers through every atom of my body. For the first time in my life, I tried my hand at prayer. I shut my eyes and muttered pleas and apologies until a white light fell on my face which I hoped was the divine light of illumination but sadly it was only the giant ugly despicable projector coming alive again.

Vandana had been picked by Royal Westend Bank. I called her mobile. "Where's the party?"

"Where are you?" She asked.

"In the Leftovers corner of the library." I tried sounding cheerful but failed miserably. "Tell me what's happening with the others."

"Sameer has landed a Sales role with Coca-Cola. Off-campus." She downplayed the importance of the message.

But I knew how much it meant to him. "Exactly what he wanted. CMO in ten years, huh? And Naina?"

"She got picked yesterday," she said after careful consideration. "America Standard. She asked me not to tell you."

"And you still did." I joked to diffuse the tension in the topic. "With friends like you, who needs enemies?"

Laboured breathing was heard on the phone as she walked down the stairs. "I am coming to see you."

"Do me a favour," I requested. "Do not."

"Ok, then here is a message," she said. "We are waiting for you on the other side. Don't for a second think you are alone. Get it?"

"Yes, thank you."

A still moment again, before she asked. "You do know who has delivered this message, don't you?"

The clunky projector blinked and sparkled again. *Bytesphere Group Discussion commences at 2 PM. All applications are being screened. Stay tuned for updates.*

"I will talk to you later," I said and hung up.

My desire to stay alone met an untimely death as I heard the chair opposite mine being dragged out, prompting me to lift my head from a cradle of sadness. Soha sat before me; she was a paler, quieter version of her former self. My disposition was such that I could not help but first pay attention to what mattered most: her hair was pulled back into a ponytail, and a crisp white shirt, buttoned up, still firmly tucked into a grey pencil skirt. Yes, she was still waiting to get a job.

Comforting as that was, I was not inclined to chitchat. "Not now, Soha."

With a hint of self-loathing, she spoke in staccato phrases. "I have brought this upon myself. Can't blame you. But, five minutes?"

"Have you got a job?" I asked. "Because I haven't."

"Fuck the job!" she thundered. I was the only member of the audience who heard the expletive. I should have been annoyed, but I could only marvel at a person who could 'fuck the job' while us lesser mortals stood yapping at selectors' heels, begging for scraps.

"Sorry." She mellowed in correction. "It's just that my mental health has been in tatters. To answer your question, no. I haven't got a job."

"Then we need to focus on something else right now," I said.

"I just want to apologise," she said.

"You are apologising to the wrong person." Geez, what on earth was happening? People whose apology I was expecting were ghosting me. Ghosts from my friend's past were randomly apologising to me. This bloody freaking air conditioner was freezing me to death. And that ominous projector was still blinking…

She cleared her throat. The rim of her nose was ruddy red from crying. "He won't talk to me. So I was hoping you could pass him the message: I had no intention to hurt him."

I could not suppress a smirk despite myself. The brazenness in the remark, if even for a moment, made me forget the crisis I was wading in. "I am sorry, there is no polite way of asking this – but what exactly was your intention when you were two-timing him?"

"I was at a phase of life I had no idea what I wanted," she said. "I don't want him back even today. I don't want to hurt anyone again. I just want to let them know I am sorry. I did some bad shit. Now I want to come clean."

The light of the projector changed hues as a volunteer tampered with the wires behind it. With a crackle it came alive again, wearing a strange magenta.

"Your name is up, Soha." I motioned towards the screen she had her back towards.

Turning around, she saw she had been shortlisted for a Cotak Bank interview on the second floor. "I can't be at peace if…"

"Go, Soha," I urged her. "Don't set out for peace at this time. No one has it in them to allow you that peace. Let this week pass by, and we will talk."

With resignation in her manner of slinking off her chair and putting her blazer back on, she said. "Yes, let the week pass by. I will wait. I just want to say that…" She looked through the window; outside on the quadrangle, Sameer and Naina stood in muted conversation. "There's only so many weeks left."

I followed her gaze even as she walked out. Sameer and Naina were now in the throes of an excited chat as a volunteer came and nodded vehemently to them in affirmation of the news. They crouched, pumped their fists in the air, and went running towards the corridor that led to the library. Midway Naina stopped and frowned, and then indicated to Sameer that he go ahead. He raised his hands in protest; she stood her ground. Before running on, he placed an arm around her shoulder in understanding. Seconds later the door of the library swung open with a thud, its knob sending a reverberation through the verticality of the wall behind it.

"Dude!" Sameer jumped over the three steps that descended onto the floor on which seventy-five study tables were placed. "You are on the Bytesphere shortlist!"

I should have guessed from the way he came running to me like a thrilled schooler. But for someone weathering a season of disappointments, receiving good news needs the same caution as inspecting a fizzled firecracker. "What does that mean?"

"Are you high?" He plucked a thumb near his lip. "It means you have a group discussion and an interview. Buckle up and look alive! Second floor in fifteen minutes. Should I get you some water? Food? Spiritual books?"

I extended a hand, letting him feel the frigid skin of my fingers. "Just good wishes."

"We are all waiting on the other side," he said, shaking my hand. "For Aryan and you. Tonight, we will all raise a toast."

I felt my limbs tremble as I scampered up four flights of stairs to reach the second floor. All floors resembled crowded flea markets with their thin corridors swamped with students: nervous candidates pacing up and down, reassured students who were already placed but were here to boost morale, co-ordinators from the junior batch, eager beavers from the junior batch who were here to witness first-hand what they'd be going through a year hence. I hopped, skipped and jumped over heads and shoulders to reach Room 21, where my group discussion was scheduled.

"Group 1 is already in," said the coordinator, reading off a sheet. "You are in Group 2. Stand by."

I could not stand by. My glands were acting up again, hence I decided to cool off in the restroom.

"What are you going in for?" asked a candidate who stood in a corner biting his fingernails.

"Bytesphere," I replied.

"Oh, that's the dream."

"Is it, now?" I asked.

Behind us, we heard a toilet bowl flush behind a closed cubicle.

"Why, is it not?"

"Not my first choice by a mile," I replied. "But you know what they say about beggars being choosers."

The toilet cubicle swung open. A plump man with sparse, grey hair emerged in a business suit and walked past me wearing a wry smile. I had half a mind to ask him if he had overheard me and if by any stroke of horrid luck, he was on the Bytesphere panel. What the hell, I would find out soon enough anyway. What more damage to my career prospects could be caused by some bathroom talk?

Minutes later I was ushered along with ten other candidates into Room 21. Eleven chairs had been placed in a semicircle. At the front sat a panel of three executives, one of whom, sure enough, was the man from the toilet cubicle. Three minutes were not enough for him to forget my face, I knew, as he passed me the same wry smile as I walked past him.

"Nice to meet you, Sir," I attempted feebly, at which he now laughed very heartily, the sadist.

"Please introduce yourselves to us first," said one of the panellists. "And then we will begin the discussion."

As the introductions rolled, I couldn't take my eyes off the Toilet Man. We locked eyes for more than a minute; it was the love story that never was. When the topic – *Technology in 2020: Where is India headed?* – was handed to us, ten candidates tore into it with urgency and ferocity. But I was still caught examining Toilet Man's challenging smirk. It was not until the fifth minute of the allotted ten that I realised I had not spoken a word. By this time the room had turned into a war zone with voices rising over each other in a bid to be heard and recognised. Never mind the cliches that were being rattled off.

"Technology is growing by leaps and bounds…"

"But we have to consider its cons…"

"India needs to channelise its resources towards humanitarian purposes to counter the effects of climate change…"

And my favourite: "I completely agree with you, but…"

I barged into the discussion with vigour and desperation, screaming my lungs out as though I was declaring a building evacuation. Toilet Man could not stop laughing. When the noise rose again as people lashed out at each other, I lifted off my seat, stretched my arms wide, and began howling my words out. For a few seconds, the panellists looked like they were going to need an ambulance. Then Toilet Man laughed again and said something to the others, pointing at me. I intensified my howling further.

"That is it, friends!" One of them banged a palm on the table twenty minutes later. "That was a very enlightening discussion."

Riding on the sarcasm of that remark, Toilet Man said, "Great to see so much passion to be a part of this company. Please wait outside and we will announce the shortlisted candidates' names very soon."

When I stepped out, my earlobes felt like embers. My breath was raspy and hurried, and with a hazy vision, I sensed Sameer standing before me, asking me questions that hit me like a Tonka truck.

"How did it go? Could you speak? Were you confident?"

"I need water," I said, sinking into a chair or whatever it was – maybe the skirting of a wall. "Get me water."

Water was sprinkled on my face and dripped on my tongue as I collected my senses. "It was ok, I guess. I can't feel my tonsils now."

Just then, Vandana came running up the stairs. "Aryan has cleared the penultimate round of Flash!"

"How many in the final round?" I asked.

"Three," she replied. "I think he is going to make it. He looked very composed."

"As should you," Sameer said, getting down on his haunches to meet my gaze. "If Aryan can, so can you. Yeah?"

I attempted a weak smile. "I don't think he will be happy to hear you say that."

"Brothers in arms," he tapped my knee.

In attestation to his prophecy, the loudspeaker spelt three names. "Paurush Vaidya, Niharika Sinha, Nakul Kapoor. Please report to the Interview Room."

"Brothers in arms!" Vandana repeated in delight, wrapping an arm around my neck.

"If I don't make it to this, I am going back home and working my farm," I said with a quiver.

"You don't own a farm."

I stood up with a sigh, drawing a heavy breath in. "Yes, so I had better make it to this."

There was but one thing stopping me. And that was my resolve to face Toilet Man. For I knew exactly what he was going to ask me.

Thus when I entered the interview room and the hushed whispers between the interviewers died upon my entry, I passed him a wry smile.

The predictable bugger asked nothing that my sixth sense had not expected. "So, Nakul. Why Bytesphere?"

It was an answer I, and surely most others in my situation would have learnt by rote. So I told him I wanted Bytesphere because of its great geographical presence, its coveted brand value, its high principles of *Parampara*, *Pratishtha*, and *Anushasan* because it treated its employees like family and so I was told. "But most importantly," I continued without pausing to breathe. "Most importantly, I align with Bytesphere's vision of changing the technological landscape of the world."

At this, one of the panel speakers burst out laughing. She must have been an MBA too; she could understand gassing when a speaker gassed. "What or who gave you the idea we are in the business of changing technological landscapes?"

"Yeah, seriously," Toilet Man chimed in. "It might seem to me your expectations from Bytesphere are very high. In all probability, you would be better off seeking higher things in life. Bytesphere should be your last choice."

Come on now, this was getting old. I stared blankly at Toilet Man as though telling him it had already become my last choice. But I could only manage to spit out some diplomatic words from a rapidly dying mouth. "I have heard great things about it."

His hands crossed over his chest, Toilet Man drummed his fingers over his arms in triumph. "Very well."

"Why don't you then tell us about your summer project?"

"Or, no," said the woman on the panel. "Let us go a little further back in time."

Don't mention Engineering. Don't mention Engineering. Don't mention...

"This robot that you say you built during your Engineering," she pondered, her finger running over one innocuous half-lie I had put on my biodata.

A half-lie because yes, a robot had been built when I was pursuing Engineering. Yes, I was on the team that built the robot. Not as an engineer, not as a robotics enthusiast, not even as a sleeping partner. I merely existed in that space and my name was on the team because my friend who was a Robotics prodigy had taken pity on me when he learnt I had no idea what I was going to do for my final semester project and had subsequently offered to let me be there.

"Just be in a corner and don't shortcircuit anything," he had said, and I had obeyed him and observed the marvels of technology as my friends fused wires, burnt midnight oil and got cranky with me every now and then. The teenager inside me had never thought an adventure like listing this achievement on a CV could get me to face a tough question two years later.

The woman shot her eyebrows right up to her hairline. "Well?"

I drew in a sharp breath, tightened my core, and vomited words that formed part of a potentially legitimate answer – except that I had no idea if I used them in the right context. "It was a wireless surveillance system with advanced manoeuvring capabilities and a micro-gripper for handling small objects and night vision..."

I slowed my words and focused my attention on their dwindling concentration. A clear win for a noob who wanted to expend little effort on the technical detail. "So, you see," I now said more confidently, "we first built a 3D CAD model, used a set of servomotors, and All we hear is Radio Gaga, Radio Googoo, Radio Gaga…"

"Ok, enough," one of them tapped their fingers on an imaginary drum; then, in contrived enthusiasm added: "That is amazing."

The sarcasm washed over me like water sliding over an oily earthen pot. *You keep the sarcasm, madam. I will take the next question, thank you.*

"So where did the robot end up getting used?" One of them asked.

"I don't really know, I am afraid," I answered.

They looked at each other, smelling triumph. "You don't come across as someone who sees one's own hard work through then, do you?"

"Oh, actually," I motioned in desperation. "I know it was picked up by a field manager at this firm in…"

Toilet Man raised his hand, asking me to stop. "Sure. So, it was accepted. That would surely make me believe you are an intelligent young man. But your grades here in B-school tell me a different story?"

It had been nineteen months until this day. Nineteen months of uncertainty, failure, dejection, and plenty of cash that had been spent on the hope that I would make something worthwhile of this premier degree. I was taking no prisoners in making sure I'd emerge from this trainwreck of a day with a job. "Sir, if I may – I don't think grades are reflective of one's true capability."

"They are not?" he asked with amusement. "Close to forty years on this planet, and I am still learning something new every day!"

"Grades do matter, Sir," I explained. "But our examination system time-boxes the assessment of our capability into three hours. That is all we get to tell our universities what we know. Give those three hours with a slow writer and terrible handwriting to a student like me, and you will see why I feel short-changed."

They looked at each other with a frown. I could not tell whether it was coated with criticism or confusion. Then one of them, who had asked me nothing in the entire interview, handed me a notepad and a pen. "Write to me in one sentence about why we should hire you."

They observed my hand to look out for signs of a nervous shiver. I gave them none. I steadied my hand as I thought for a few seconds before writing: "I am a great team player who will have a lot to learn from the seniors in your organisation. In return, I can assure them of my hunger to learn and a drive to excel at my work."

He peered into my answer and laughed. "Yes, you really do have terrible handwriting!"

Toilet Man took a pen out of his shirt pocket, pulled the notepad, scribbled something and pushed it back to me. *Would you like to join us in June this year?*

I ran a tongue over my parched mouth. Conscious of the sound of my heartbeat, I breathed hard. My vision at first strained; seconds later, my eyes relaxed, soaked at the moment as I read and re-read every letter, every curve of his equally terrible handwriting.

The words were interlocked between my open jaws. I managed but a nod, desperately hopeful the tears would not stream out just then.

They shook hands with me and smiled. "We will dispatch the offer letter by post."

I bolted out, holding the tears until I was out of their sight. They came hurtling down my cheeks when my friends crowded around me, but I had already bared my soul before them. I was in a safe space.

"What happened?" Sameer asked, holding me by the shoulder.

I gasped for breath. "They – they are dispatching the offer letter – by post."

Naina and Vandana had now entered the huddle. All of them broke into a congratulatory roar. But this all still felt too surreal.

"So," I spoke with a shiver. "It does mean I got the job, right?"

"Are you crazy?" They screamed. "Of course, that is what it means!"

"Must check," I rambled as I opened the door to go back in even as the others tried stopping me in vain.

"May I?" I asked peeping in.

They could tell I had had a bit of a cry. "Is everything fine?"

"Just double checking, sorry," I said. "Am I…"

They laughed. "You are hired, Nakul."

This time I exited the room with a chuckle, embarrassed by my own behaviour. "Yeah, I did get the job!"

Naina stepped forward and shook my hand. Even in celebration, the fracture in friendship was evident. Handshakes had officially replaced hugs. "Congratulations, Nakul."

"How did you go?" I asked her, accepting the handshake.

"America Standard," she answered with a smile.

"The best!" I marvelled. "Hardly surprising. You deserved the best."

"It calls for a celebration," she said. Presently, another student in the adjacent room had got placed. A loud applause broke out. She waited for the clamour to die. "Coffee and cake?"

It was a hark back to the times when trust was assumed, not promised. I wanted to say yes, but the fool in me said that one month was sufficient runway to continue holding a grudge, wait to be chased up on resolving it and then reliving the old, better moments that did not have the baggage of complaint. "Damn right, Naina. You must go celebrate with coffee and cake."

I slinked away with complete knowledge that I was being a prude. Half-expecting her to run after me and call dibs on sorting matters, I slowed my steps but I could not so much as see my own shadow snapping at my heels. Down the next flight of stairs, a loud cry broke out.

One! Two! Three!

No, stop, ok that's it!

Laughter.

…Nine! And ten!

I glided down to see Aryan sprawled on the marble floor, writhing in pain yet smiling with ecstasy.

"Go put some Vaseline now, champ!" One from the crowd said before the crowd dispersed.

I offered him a hand. He smiled weakly. "I made it to Flash Consumer Durables!"

"I made it to Bytesphere," I said victoriously, hauling him up to his feet. "Ten minutes before you!"

"Shall we discuss our life plans again, now?" He asked.

"For now, let us just get out of here."

28

Few things must explain longing like a campus rendered desolate after having been a stomping ground for a jamboree. With jobs in their hands, students could not care less about attendance for the last four weeks. People had caught either the first train home to be with their families or the first bus to Goa to get sloshed in happiness. Flyers about the farewell party and the convocation ceremony had begun to get distributed. They smelt of departure and heartache.

"I feel sick staring at these trees," I winced. "We should have gone to Goa too."

Sameer gritted his teeth, letting white smoke off his cigarette escape in a wisp. "I had offered it. You vetoed the idea."

"It was too expensive."

"It was not," he said. "You and I both know why you declined it."

I took a drag off his cigarette and looked at him for guidance. He motioned with a deep inhalation followed by a slow exhalation. I did as told, but the smoke got trapped in my throat, pushing me into a violent bout of cough.

He snatched his possession back and shook his head, taking another puff. "Why the hell would you try a shitty thing you have never laid your hands on?"

"Being a good boy has not paid great dividends," I laughed. "I could do with a few shitty habits now."

He shook his head in disapproval. "You must stay a good boy."

I nodded. There was something I wanted to talk to him about. I had felt a complete lack of motivation towards it until now. I still felt it. But I just had to vomit it out before we were out of there. "Then I will let you in on something. With some advice. Because that is what good boys do." I had his attention. "Soha came to me the other day. The girl is a total mess and is deeply remorseful."

He offered a light shrug. "And what is your advice?"

"That you should bury the hatchet," I said. "Because that is what good boys do."

"You reckon?" He second-guessed me. "Because you don't seem great at burying the hatchet."

The cigarette had left a terrible aftertaste. *Never again,* I told myself. Popping a mint, I nodded. "I know. But you are a better person than me. With a larger heart and a smaller ego. You can do this."

"I met Soha this morning," he told me. "I had no idea she had spoken to you. We just bumped into each other in the hallway. I stopped her and we spoke."

"And?"

"Just general stuff," he waved his palm side to side. "Wishing each other for the future. She began to offer an apology, and I told her it was not required."

"See?" I smiled. "I told you – you are large-hearted."

He shook his head. "I did it for myself, Nakul. I can't carry the burden of judging a person for so long. Yes, I would never do to anyone what she did to me. But I can't force her to be like me. I know this is a lesson hard to swallow, but it is a simple truth: we are all different, and we have a right to be so."

He studied my distant gaze. "A penny for your thoughts?"

I fumbled through my pockets, my weak attempt at humour to cover up for what I was actually thinking. "I have none." Not one muscle on his face moved to smile. "I will heed your words. I will email her too – an email to close all differences."

"What are you?" He looked at me with disdain. "Her stalker? Her lover? Her distant cousin? If you are none of these, you shouldn't be sending her an email. Go front up to her and talk it out like friends do. Enough of this email nonsense already."

"Yes, alright," I conceded, half-hoping this encounter would not come to pass. "I will talk to her when I see her."

"She went out to the sandwich stall with Vandana ten minutes ago," he motioned towards the gate. "There, I have solved half the problem for you. Now let me see if you are a man of your word."

I walked out with feet colder than I had when I had entered that unpleasant interview room. Looking for her weakly, I felt an oncoming headache and definite queasiness. The kerb lining the fast-food stalls was fittingly quiet for a Sunday. I rested against a lorry parked diagonally against it, contemplating a *lassi* to combat the headache as well as the queasiness. Accepting a bottle in exchange for a tenner, I heard the first recognisable sound besides my own loud slurps of the drink. I knew the voices; they came from the other side of the lorry.

"I can handle discord if it comes from differences of opinion," said Naina in response to something she had been asked. "It is the judgement that troubles me."

"He has a different point of view on this, surely," said Vandana. "You don't have to agree with him. But go and sort out your differences at least."

A loud hum of a passing autorickshaw posed an interruption. Then Naina's voice rose again. "It takes two to tango. I have tried stepping forward to talk. To explain myself – even though I have felt I must not need to. But he…he just won't talk. After a few tries, it has become exhausting."

"I wish this could end differently," rued Vandana. "Listen – can I play mediator? Should I arrange a clandestine meeting far from the madding crowd? You two can slap some sense into one another amidst some quietude if that could help?"

Laughter followed. Then, another rickshaw trundled past, carrying the weight of three hefty passengers that was compensated by one leg of the driver dangling outward.

"The little girl has become wise enough to play mediator right after landing her first job?" Naina teased her. "No, you must not. What good will come of it anyway? We slap some sense into one another, give one another a hug of apology, and then two days later he will be upset about something again. No, V. We are wired too differently."

"So, are you ready to lose a friend?"

The long silence after the question knocked the remaining wind out of my sails. I put the drink down.

"Why would I lose a friend?" she said finally. "I would hold on to it like a fine wine that ages with time, yes? Time is the best healer. When we meet again – whenever that is – I am sure we will have moved on a long way forward from the problems of today."

When we meet again. I smiled despite myself as I walked away for one final time.

As an ode to the smooth sands of time,
Is a promise equal parts foolhardy and sublime,
Vast as might be our distances to gain.
We will turn back the clock when we meet again.
Whiffs of these memories will sweep at our feet,
Through a lyric, a limerick, or a coffee shop receipt
That will push us down a bittersweet memory lane,
Those were the days, we will sigh when we meet again.

As I wound around the road in a slow walk back to the hostel, I saw a small group of students from the junior batch sipping on *cutting chais* at the tea stall. They were where I once was: reckless and happy, and foolish to imagine they had found a perfect universe that would stay unchanged. Now that I stood at the exit of this Utopian journey, I thought I should have felt a pang of jealousy looking at them. But nothing of the sort happened. I levitated on a little cloud, wherefrom I looked down upon the Utopian world of *great times with friends who are family.* I felt a syringe of indifference course through my veins. And that day, finally, I felt *Comfortably Numb.*

29

My room was in shambles. Two jumbo suitcases stood in a corner, covered with cobwebs and cakes of dust accumulated over time. Like two soldiers on a long R&R who were now ready to be deployed. Stacks of clothes lay on the bed. A steel almirah that bore my name with a yellowed, peeling sticker now lay nearly empty save for a few scattered papers: the graded and rejected assignments would go in the bin, and notes that carried silly scribbles during lectures were retained as keepsakes. The clock on the table ticked away ominously. Two hours to the convocation, six hours to be an ex-student.

It was a merciless scorcher of an April afternoon. Add to that a black convocation cloak strung around the neck and business suits underneath, and we were all toast. We stood in a formation of two rows outside the hall, waiting for the dignitaries to arrive. Leading from the front was a band of musicians in white uniforms, loaded with trumpets and huge drums.

"I don't remember feeling this important before," Aryan said. "Sure feels good! Except this, of course." He soaked sweat off his forehead onto a handkerchief.

"It only gets better," Sameer patted him. "Very soon you will be in that."

He motioned towards a silver Mercedes that now pulled in through the VIP gate. The chief guest – the President of a multinational bank that picked three of our brightest minds – was greeted by members of the Students' Council, the Dean and the Vice-Chancellor. Garlands and bouquets were handed before he was whisked away through the rear door. The band now started beating its drums and trumpets, leading us into the hall one march at a time. When we entered the dark, airconditioned hall after an eternity, the fresh blast of air from the vents overhead felt like paradise. The assembly had been choreographed down to the finest detail. The two rows would split at the centre, each student was well-versed in their position in the auditorium. In one swift scoop, cloaks shuffled, shoes tapped, and bums rested on the hard plastic seats.

Ruchi Karwal met me halfway along the aisle leading to my chair. "Where did you get your posting?" she whispered.

"Hyderabad," I replied. "Is it a nice place?"

"Must be," she shrugged. "I have never been there."

"You should," I suggested. "So you can find out."

She smiled with radiance as she always did. "I didn't give you my number, did I?"

"Shh," a party-pooping volunteer admonished us from the hallway with a finger pressed to his lips. "The proceedings are about to begin."

And hence, ours would have to wait. She slipped me her number on my phone, flashed me a smile and a goodbye wave, and disappeared several rows behind. The last of the lights in the hall now went off and a floodlight appeared on the dais as the chief guest was accompanied to centre stage by the Dean, the Vice-Chancellor, and a flurry of trustees each of whom would deliver a speech of equal length and intensity. We endured the speeches in anticipation of being handed out our degree certificates as each one of us was summoned to the stage. The euphoria of receiving the degree had nothing on the moment when the convocation ceremony was declared closed. Two hundred delighted souls sprang to their feet and tossed their hats in the air. The batch broke into a deafening roar, followed by a round of congratulatory embraces.

I felt a hand on my shoulder. "I have my flight at six," Vandana said, looking at me with teary eyes. "I am headed straight to the airport."

The finality of the moment coursed through me with the pace of an anaesthetic. "You did not tell me. I thought we could have sat down for a satisfying last chat."

She gave me a long, comforting hug. Pulling back, she said. "There is no such thing as a satisfying last chat, my friend. We had rather rip off the band-aid now."

"Let me walk you to a cab," I offered.

We saw Naina advance down the hallway. "No, you should not," Vandana said to me. "Stay. And by the way, this was *not* the last chat!"

She slinked away before I knew it. Thereon exits from the auditorium and our lives occurred every few minutes, like the final remnants of a sandcastle being pushed at by a wave.

"Do you have time for a last drink?" Sameer came up to me. "One each at Enigma, and then you head straight to the station? Aryan and Swapnil are in."

"We will need to go to the hostel first," I said slowly, unsure if I wanted to stay or leave. "Pack our bags, and then…"

He found me looking at Naina. "Or if you want to stay here and meet others once, cool with me."

Until we meet again, I said to myself. "No, I am good," I looked at him. "Let us leave."

The turnout at the pub was thin. Only two tables other than ours were occupied. The band that usually regaled us with live music was absent today – an atmosphere that befitted the disquiet that we felt. It felt like the longest drinking session with the littlest exchange of words.

Until Swapnil noted the time on his watch and rapped a knuckle on the table. "I think you need to run along."

"Must I?" I looked at my watch and sat up, alarmed. "Oh yes, run along I must!"

"Let us get you a cab," they walked out with me.

We stood at the kerb for five minutes until a taxi pulled over. "I think we must plan a trip."

"Like a reunion," Aryan suggested. "A six-month reunion."

"He needs six months to recover from our company," Swapnil laughed.

"Let us leave him out," I joked. "The rest of us can plan one this month."

"Goa?"

"Anywhere," I said.

"Bali," suggested Swapnil. "And then another one in six months when Aryan can join."

"Yeah, yeah," Aryan shook his head, "whatever."

"That one can be in Matheran," Sameer laughed. "We won't be able to afford two international trips in a year."

When the laughter subsided and the taxi driver indicated he did not have all evening to entertain our maudlin promises, I plonked into the rear seat. The engine kicked up a cloud of smoke and blurred their silhouettes. With the dissolution of the smoke also went the final visual of a treasure trove of memories. As I looked straight ahead, Bombay suddenly morphed into another ordinary city – far from the paradise I had romanticised it to be – that choked me with its bumps and potholes and abundant traffic jams.

"What time is your train?" asked the driver.

"Nine-something," I replied absently.

"It is nine-something already," he said. "You will be lucky if you don't miss it."

He screeched to a halt at the rear end of Dadar Station. I handed him the fare and bolted without bothering to receive the change. I could not bear being in this city for another night if I were to miss this train. The first whistle sounded on Platform 11. I glided up and down the footbridge and by the time the second whistle went off, I had smelt the upholstery of the three-tier AC bogey. At the third whistle, I had deposited myself clumsily on the side berth and clutched at my chest to catch my breath. It is then that my phone rang.

'Naina calling', the screen displayed.

I answered shakily. "Hello?"

She spoke slowly, with hesitation and sadness. "Have you left?"

The train rumbled to a slow start. "Just. I just made it, but yes. I have left."

A firm disappointment rang in her voice. There was a sense of authority to her demand, something I wish I had seen a little earlier. "I thought I deserved one meeting before you took off."

"Of course, you do," I answered. "I wanted to. But I was rushed."

"Never knew you to be the person who was too rushed to have a word with a friend," she said with a hint of accusation.

The train had gained momentum. Within minutes as long as the pregnant pauses in our conversation, it had exited the mainland and was making its way into the outskirts. The telephone line began to crackle as I saw the network on my signal dip slowly but surely.

"I know it is too late to say this," she said. "But I wish…we…not drifted…"

"Are you still there?" I yelled into the phone. "You are breaking up."

"I still value…" I heard syllables and broken words. "Don't know how…haywire…we can still resolve…"

"Hello?"

"I don't…end things…," she shouted. "Hello? Are you with me?"

The network bars finally dipped to zero. On the screen, a message flashed: *Out of coverage.*